A Novel by N. Alessandro Penington

SNOWFLAKE AND THE ENCHANTED SEVEN

ISBN: 978-1-965273-04-3 (Paperback)

Library of Congress Control Number: 2024949750

Any references to historical events, real people, or real places are used fictitiously. Names, characters, and places are products of the author's imagination.

Front cover image by Perez MMG Publishing

Book design by Perez MMG Publishing

Printed in United States of America First printing edition 2024.

Seerendip Publishing
SeerendipPublishing.com

$$|\psi\rangle = (1/\sqrt{2})(|00\rangle + |11\rangle)$$

Contents

Prologue

With her otherworldly beauty and enigmatic presence, Snowflake was born of enchantment and tragedy. Her arrival in the lives of the seven little dwarves was no coincidence but a convergence of fate and a longing for a place to call home. She brought an aura of mystique, her every step accompanied by a faint glimmer of magic that danced in the air around her.

In her past life, Snowflake had been a patron of a far-off realm known as Crystalia, a place of wonder and marvels. Crystalia was a world where magic flowed like a river, its currents of power swirling and intertwining. As the daughter of a powerful sorceress who held sway over the elements, Snowflake had grown up surrounded by shimmering ice sculptures, and the ethereal melodies of her mother's enchantments. With a mere flick of her fingers, Snowflake could conjure delicate frost patterns that adorned the air with their intricate beauty.

But Crystalia, with all its grandeur, was not immune to darkness. A malevolent force had begun to seep into the realm, its tendrils of shadows threatening to snuff out the essence of magic itself. Snowflake witnessed the gradual decay of her beloved homeland, its vibrant hues giving way to shades of gray. The delicate balance of the world was teetering on the edge of oblivion.

In a final act of sacrifice, Snowflake's mother, a sorceress of unparalleled power, harnessed the last remnants of her magic to open a mystical portal. With tear-filled eyes, she urged her daughter to flee, to seek refuge in a realm untouched by the encroaching darkness. It was a desperate attempt to save her child from the impending doom that awaited Crystalia.

As Snowflake emerged from the portal, she found herself in an enchanted forest, a sanctuary of ancient trees and whispering leaves. She stood in awe, marveling at the vibrant tapestry of colors and the delicate symphony of nature surrounding her. The air was thick with the scent of wildflowers and the gentle murmur of hidden streams.

Alone and bereft, Snowflake wandered through the forest, her heart heavy with grief and longing for her lost home. The weight of the world's crumbling magic burdened her spirit, but she remained determined to find solace and purpose amidst the unknown.

During her wanderings, seven dwarves, renowned throughout the land for their indomitable spirit and kind hearts, discovered her. Their paths crossed serendipitously; their destinies intertwined in a way that defied logic. Drawn to Snowflake's ethereal presence and the flicker of sorrow in her eyes, they extended a hand of friendship and offered her a place within their humble abode.

Inside the cozy haven of their cottage, Snowflake found respite from her wandering, her icy demeanor thawing in the warmth of their acceptance. The dwarves, with their weathered faces and calloused hands, became her steadfast protectors and guardians, embracing her as a beloved member of their tightly knit family. Together, they forged a bond built on trust, resilience, and a shared appreciation for the beauty of the natural world.

The dwarves, touched by Snowflake's enchanting grace and innate goodness, marveled at the transformation within her. Her radiant smile became a beacon of light, capable of dispelling even the darkest shadows that threatened their peaceful existence. And in return,

Snowflake cherished the dwarves' unwavering loyalty and steadfast presence, finding solace in their unspoken understanding of the pain that lingered in her heart.

Though Snowflake rarely spoke of her past, the dwarves could sense the weight of her loss, the remnants of a shattered world that occasionally flickered in her gaze. They offered her a space where memories found voice, tears could be shed, and laughter resonated through the halls of their cozy home. They knew healing was gradual, so they stood by her side, providing a foundation of love and support.

Snowflake's connection to the forest around her with each passing day deepened. The trees seemed to lean in closer, whispering secrets and ancient wisdom to her. The creatures of the forest, from the timid rabbits to the majestic deer, recognized her as a benevolent force, seeking her guidance and protection.

In the twilight of the enchanted forest, Snowflake's past remained haunting, but it no longer defined her. She had found a new family, a new purpose, and a profound sense of belonging. The seven dwarves, with their resilience and loyalty, had opened their hearts and home to her, forever altering the course of her destiny.

CHAPTER ONE

The sun's golden rays filtered through the vibrant leaves of the ancient trees, casting a warm and ethereal glow upon the enchanted forest. In a secluded clearing, nestled amidst a tapestry of wildflowers and moss-covered stones, stood a quaint wooden hut. It was adorned with delicate carvings of woodland creatures and exuded an air of magic and whimsy.

Inside the cozy hut, Snowflake moved gracefully about the kitchen, her porcelain skin glowing with an otherworldly radiance. Her black hair cascaded in loose waves down her back, complementing her enchanting violet eyes. Clad in a flowing emerald gown adorned with silver embroidery, she hummed a gentle melody as she prepared a sumptuous feast for her companions.

Seven little dwarves, Grumble, Swift, Glimmer, Puddle, Snicker, Bristle, and Whisker, sat around a sturdy wooden table, their weathered faces etched with tales of adventure and laughter. Each dwarf possessed unique characteristics that made them easily distinguishable.

Grumble, the eldest and most gruff of the group, had a massive bushy beard that nearly obscured his face. His deep voice resonated through the hut as he regaled the others with stories of their mining expeditions. His hands, calloused from years of hard work, held a sense of rugged strength.

Swift, the youngest of the dwarves, was nimble and quick-footed. With a perpetual look in his eyes, he possessed an energy that never failed to lift the spirits of those around him. His lean frame and never-ending motion spoke of his constant curiosity.

Glimmer, known for his radiant smile, was the eternal optimist. His presence lit up the room, and his words carried a lightheartedness that never failed to bring a smile to the faces of his companions. His fair complexion seemed to shimmer with an inner glow, mirroring his positive outlook on life.

Puddle, the jolly prankster of the group, had a round belly and a hearty laugh that filled the room. He often delighted in playing harmless tricks on his fellow dwarves, always ensuring that laughter was a constant presence in their lives. His rosy cheeks and twinkling eyes reflected his mischievous nature.

Snicker was known for his peculiar sense of humor. His laughter bubbled up at the most unexpected and often inappropriate times. His face, adorned with a short, unruly beard, seemed to betray his impish nature.

Bristle, with his wild mane of hair and beard, was the group's resident storyteller. His deep, rumbling voice captivated all who listened as he weaved tales of legends and lore. His rough exterior concealed a heart filled with wisdom and an insatiable curiosity about the world beyond their forest home.

Whisker, the most innocent-looking of the dwarves, had a face covered in a fuzz of golden hair. His wide eyes were filled with wonder and awe as he absorbed every detail of their surroundings. He possessed a childlike innocence that reminded the others of the magic in the world.

As Snowflake bustled around the kitchen, the aroma of delicious food wafted through the air, mingling with the gentle crackling of the fire in the hearth. The dwarves' stomachs rumbled in anticipation, and they couldn't help but exchange playful banter as they eagerly awaited their meal. Grumble, scratching his scruffy beard, chuckled heartily. "And then, just as we thought we'd hit gold, ol' Swift here tripped over his own feet and sent us all tumbling down the shaft!"

Swift's cheeks flushed with embarrassment, but he couldn't help but laugh at the memory. "Hey now, it's not my fault the ground was uneven! Besides, we all had a good laugh after the dust settled."

Glimmer chimed in, his twinkling eyes reflecting the flickering light of the hearth. "Well, the silver lining was that we discovered that vein right below! It was like a gift from the forest itself!"

Puddle, the jovial prankster, playfully teased Snicker. "You've got that permanent grin, Snicker. It's a wonder your face doesn't crack!"

Snicker chuckled and shrugged. "What can I say? I can't help but find joy in every little thing. Life's too short not to smile."

Bristle, always eager to share a tale, leaned forward, his voice filled with excitement. "You know, we once encountered a group of mischievous sprites during one of our mining expeditions. They kept hiding our tools and replacing them with rocks! Took us ages to catch on!"

Amidst the cheerful chatter, Snowflake paused in her culinary endeavors and joined the conversation. "Your stories always bring light to my heart. Now, let me tell you what delicious treats I have in store for tonight's feast. I've prepared a mouthwatering venison stew, fragrant herb bread, and a delightful berry tart for dessert."

The dwarves' eyes lit up with anticipation, and they playfully jostled each other in their eagerness to be seated at the table. Snowflake's laughter filled the air as she gracefully served each dish, her delicate hands moving with mesmerizing grace.

As the group savored the meal, their laughter, and merriment filled the hut, creating a joyful ambiance that seemed to harmonize with the enchanting surroundings. The air was filled with the tantalizing scents of the food, and the dwarves' hearty appetites were sated with each delicious bite.

However, as the group indulged in the delectable meal, a sudden shift in the atmosphere caught their attention. The air grew heavy as if a veil of anticipation settled upon the forest. The cheerful chatter died down, and the dwarves exchanged curious glances.

Snowflake's heart quickened with curiosity. Her keen senses tingled with awareness, and she couldn't help but comment on the sudden change in the forest.

"Do you feel that?" Snowflake's voice carried a note of concern as she glanced at her dwarf companions. "It's eerie, isn't it? The forest, it's usually buzzing with whispers and melodies, but now... it's like everything's gone quiet, as if it's holding its breath, waiting for something."

The dwarves, their expressions filled with a mixture of curiosity and apprehension, exchanged worried glances. Grumble, his bushy eyebrows furrowed, spoke up, voicing their collective thoughts. "Aye, Snowflake, I can feel it too. Something ain't right. I've never heard the forest so still. It could be an approaching storm, but I've got a feeling there's more to it."

Swift rose from his chair and strode over to the window. He gazed out onto the once serene landscape, his keen eyes scanning the surroundings.

A furrow creased his brow as he took in the scene before him. As a dark cloud descended over the trees, the very essence of the forest seemed to quiver with unnatural energy. The leaves wilted, their vibrant greens turning dull and lifeless. Flowers drooped, their petals losing their radiant colors. Even the ancient tree trunks bore a weary and withered appearance as if burdened by an unseen force.

Swift also couldn't help but notice the absence of the gentle creatures that usually frequented the clearing. The deer, usually grazing peacefully nearby, were nowhere to be seen. It was as if they had vanished, leaving behind only a sense of emptiness. He had seen Snowflake earlier, generously providing the forest animals with delectable treats, but now the rabbits had retreated into their burrows, their little noses poking out only to sniff the air cautiously. The birds, once melodiously serenading the forest with their songs, had taken refuge in the protective branches, their chirps replaced by an eerie silence.

"They're all gone," Swift muttered, his voice tinged with worry. "The deer, the rabbits, the birds. They're all hiding as if they sense something amiss in the air. It's not like them to disappear so suddenly, especially after being treated to Snowflake's kindness."

His companions leaned in, their expressions mirroring his concern. Glimmer, his eyes filled with empathy, placed a comforting hand on Swift's shoulder. "The creatures of these woods are attuned to nature's rhythms, and they can sense danger before we do."

Grumble grumbled under his breath, "Can't say I blame 'em for hidin'. We need to find out what's causin' this."

Puddle interjected with a touch of unease in his voice. "Perhaps it's a rare phenomenon, a natural occurrence we've yet to witness. Although, I must admit, it feels more foreboding than any natural event I've encountered before."

Snicker suggested, "Maybe it's a reenactment of trouble like the legends of old. The forest protects itself, perhaps, and this is its way of warding off a danger we can't perceive."

Bristle added, "There are ancient tales of cursed enchantments, where malevolent forces consume the very life force of the land. Could this be one of those tales brought to life?"

The dwarves exchanged glances; their expressions filled with worry. With a collective agreement, they rose from their chairs, their sturdy boots echoing softly on the wooden floor.

Grumble, being the eldest and most protective, turned towards Snowflake, his voice filled with concern. "You stay inside, lass. We'll go out and see what in the blazes is goin' on. No need for you to put yourself in harm's way."

Snowflake nodded her expression a mixture of worry and trust. "Be careful."

With a final reassuring smile, the dwarves donned their cloaks and headed toward the front door. Stepping outside, they were immediately greeted by an unsettling sight. The once-vibrant forest had been cast into shadow, the sunlight struggling to pierce through the encroaching darkness.

Swift, his eyes scanning the ominous scene, whispered under his breath, "By the beards of our ancestors, this is no natural occurrence. I've never seen anything like it in all my years. Perhaps your folktale is not far off from the truth."

As they gazed toward the approaching darkness, a subtle symphony of enchantment unfolded before their eyes. Swirling motes of fairy dust sparkled in the air, catching the light, and forming intricate patterns that wove through the surrounding trees. The tiny specks of luminescence seemed to whisper secrets of forgotten times, evoking a sense of awe and anticipation.

A gentle breeze, carrying the echoes of magic, caressed the dwarves' faces. It whispered through the leaves, carrying with it a melody of arcane knowledge and hidden powers. The delicate touch of the wind seemed to invite the dwarves to the mystery, urging them to delve deeper into the unknown.

Glimmer, his voice filled with a mixture of awe and trepidation, added, "Look at the way the cloud moves as if it has a mind of its own. It's not a storm, that's for certain. This is something far more... sinister."

Just as they were about to devise a plan, the shadows abruptly shifted. A bolt of dark energy shot forth from the heart of the cloud, crackling with unholy power. It struck the ground mere inches away from the dwarves, causing the earth to tremble beneath their feet.

At that moment, time seemed to freeze. The dwarves stared wide-eyed at the smoldering impact point, their hearts racing with a newfound urgency. They were confronted with a harsh reality—they were now directly in the path of a force that could potentially threaten their lives and everything they held dear.

In that moment of impending danger, the dwarves' survival instincts ignited like a blazing fire within their chests. Their faces, etched with fear and determination, reflected the flickering light of the hearth as they darted back toward their cozy cottage. Each hurried step reverberated through the forest; their echoing footfalls were like a haunting chorus that harmonized with the rising tension in the air.

With trembling hands, they swung the heavy wooden door shut, the sound of its closing, shook through the silence with a resolute finality. The door, now a fortress against the encroaching darkness, served as a tangible barrier between the safety of their sanctuary and the ominous unknown beyond.

Gathered in a tight circle, the dwarves formed an unyielding shield around Snowflake, their stalwart frames encircling her like a shield of steady loyalty. The atmosphere crackled with a potent blend of fear and anticipation.

Their eyes, darting from window to window, searched for any glimpse of what awaited them beyond the safety of their fortified walls. Through the small panes of glass, they caught fleeting glimpses of the forest, its once vibrant tapestry now shrouded in an unsettling gloom. Shadows danced with eerie grace, their movements mirroring the swirling tendrils of darkness that emanated from the cloud.

The room itself seemed to constrict, its walls closing in with a palpable sense of protection. The rustic beams overhead, once a comforting reminder of the sturdy shelter they had built, now served as a reminder of the imminent danger that loomed just beyond their reach. The hearth, now a flickering island of warmth, cast dancing shadows on their faces, accentuating the lines of worry etched upon their weathered features.

As the dark cloud pressed closer, its presence seeping into every crevice of their existence, the dwarves exchanged solemn glances. Unspoken words passed between them as they braced for the dark cloud that settled over the hut like a blanket smothering its occupant…

cbapter two

With their weary steps echoing in the dense silence of the forest's edge, Ava led the group onward, her determination unyielding despite the weariness etched into her features. For what felt like days, they had trudged through the wilderness, their journey fraught with obstacles and uncertainty. The towering trees loomed ominously ahead, their twisted branches casting long shadows that stretched across the forest floor.

As they approached the threshold of the enchanted woods, a sense of foreboding settled over them like a heavy shroud. The air grew thick with an otherworldly stillness, the oppressive weight of the forest pressing down upon their weary souls. Shafts of fading sunlight filtered through the dense canopy, casting dappled patterns of light and shadow upon the ground.

"We must proceed with caution," Ava's voice broke the silence, her words a solemn reminder of the dangers that lurked within the depths of the forest. "The path ahead is treacherous, and we know not what awaits us within."

Ben nodded in agreement, his gaze fixed upon the dark expanse of trees ahead. "Agreed," he murmured, his voice tinged with grim resolve. "But we cannot afford to falter now. The fate of the realm hangs in the balance."

Tico exchanged a worried glance with the others, his brow furrowed with concern. "We've come too far to turn back now," he said, his voice low and determined. "But we must remain vigilant. The forest holds many dangers, and we cannot afford to underestimate them."

Holly clutched the strap of her satchel tightly, her eyes wide with apprehension. "I-I'm scared," she admitted softly, her voice trembling with uncertainty. "But we have to keep going, right?"

Ava reached out to gently squeeze Holly's hand, offering her a reassuring smile. "We're in this together," she said, her voice steady and resolute. "And together, we will find the answers we seek."

With a collective breath, the group stepped forward into the looming shadows of the enchanted forest, their hearts heavy with the weight of their mission. And as they disappeared into the darkness, the forest seemed to swallow them whole, its secrets shrouded in an eerie silence that echoed through the ancient trees.

Ava led the group through the dense thicket of the enchanted forest. Her flowing chestnut hair cascaded over her shoulders, framing her face with a touch of quiet determination. She exuded an aura of calm and rationality, her voice resonating with a soothing clarity that reassured her companions.

Walking beside Ava was Ben, his tall and muscular frame is a testament to his courage and strength. His piercing blue eyes, filled with unwavering sense of purpose, scanned the surroundings with an unshakable focus. Clad in rugged attire and carrying a sturdy staff, he was the embodiment of bravery, always ready to face whatever challenges lay ahead.

Tico, a compact and agile figure, walked a few steps behind, ever watchful of the group's safety. His olive skin and deep-set eyes reflected his loyalty and protective nature. With each step, his ears perked up, keenly attuned to the subtle whispers of the forest.

Tico's presence provided a sense of security, and his skill in navigating the wilderness was invaluable to the group's journey.

Holly, the youngest of the group, had a delicate grace about her. Her golden curls danced in the sunlight, framing her innocent face. Her hazel eyes sparkled with curiosity, but a hint of vulnerability lingered beneath her seemingly carefree demeanor. While she possessed an independent spirit, her timid nature often made her susceptible to fear. Yet, her presence brought the group a sense of wonder and joy, a reminder of the beauty that still thrived amidst the eerie surroundings.

As they ventured deeper into the forest, the air grew thick with an otherworldly ambiance. Shafts of sunlight filtered through the thick canopy, casting ethereal beams that danced upon the forest floor. The vibrant and lush foliage seemed to possess a conscious quality, rustling, and whispering secrets as the group passed.

Magical elements intertwined with the forest's natural beauty. Delicate flowers with petals that glimmered like stardust bloomed along the path, their subtle fragrance filling the air with an intoxicating sweetness. Moss-covered stones hummed with ancient enchantments, their vibrant hues shifting and changing in a mesmerizing display.

Yet, amidst the enchantment, an underlying sense of unease pervaded the forest. The towering trees seemed to lean menacingly, their gnarled branches reaching out like skeletal fingers. Shadows danced and flickered, taking on eerie forms that tested the limits of imagination. Whispers echoed through the thick foliage, carrying both enchanting melodies and foreboding warnings.

As the group continued their trek, Ava's steady and relentless voice cut through the tension. "Keep your senses sharp. This forest is filled with both beauty and danger."

Ben tightened his grip on his staff, his gaze locked ahead. "It's the danger I am worried about."

Tico cast a vigilant gaze in every direction, his presence a shield of protection. "As long as we stay together, we'll be alright."

Holly, though apprehensive, mustered her courage and added, "This forest hides something dark. I can feel it."

Ava, her brows furrowed in deep thought, spoke first. "The dark magic seems to be shifting, elusive and unpredictable. We have to be vigilant, for it has the power to infiltrate the very fabric of this forest. Its influence can alter the behavior of creatures and distort the natural order. We cannot afford to underestimate its reach."

"Agreed." Tico added, His gaze darting from shadow to shadow, "We have witnessed some strange occurrences lately, and the forest itself seems restless as if it senses the encroaching darkness. We must be prepared for the unexpected and keep an eye out for any signs of disruption."

Ben, gripping his staff tighter, interjected with a resolute tone. "The dark magic may be cunning, but our determination is stronger.

Holly, her voice carrying a touch of trepidation, chimed in, "But what if the dark magic affects us as well? What if it clouds our judgment or twists our intentions?"

"That won't happen. Not if we have each other's backs," Tico promised.

The forest grew dense with an eerie silence as Ben, Ava, Holly, and Tico ventured deeper into its shadowy depths. The oppressive presence of the dark magic hung heavy in the air, heightening their senses, and filling their hearts with unease. Unbeknownst to them, their footsteps stirred a pack of supernatural wolves, creatures twisted by the malevolent influence of dark magic.

As the team continued their trek, a low growl reverberated through the trees, sending shivers down their spines. Glowing red eyes pierced the darkness, and a pack of wolves emerged from the shadows, their fangs bared in a menacing display of aggression. Their fur bristled, and their predatory instincts sharpened, hungry for the taste of intruders who dared to trespass upon their territory.

Ava's voice quivered slightly as she whispered, "These wolves are no doubt affected by the magic floating around here."

Holly's hands trembled, but she steadied her breathing, determined not to let fear consume her. "What are we going to do, Ava? They seem relentless, ready to tear us apart."

Ben, his bravery shining through his eyes, surveyed their surroundings. "There must be a weakness. The dark magic may have enhanced their senses and agility, but if we can distract them for a few seconds, we might stand a chance."

Ava's hand instinctively clutched the necklace adorning her neck—a precious heirloom passed down through generations. It housed a crystal pendant that shimmered with an inner radiance. "I have an idea. My necklace contains a powerful crystal that emits a magical bright light. What if we can temporarily blind the wolves?"

Tico, his voice resolute, nodded in agreement. "And while they're disoriented, we can make a run for it."

With a shared determination, they enacted their plan. Ava, focusing on the magic within, unclasped the necklace, unleashing its brilliant glow, and illuminating the darkness. The wolves recoiled, their eyes narrowing against the blinding light. Seizing the moment, Ben, Holly, and Tico bolted.

Heartbeats thundering in their ears, the team ran with wild recklessness through the dense forest, their footsteps pounding against the earth desperately trying to outpace the pursuit of the supernatural wolves. Each step propelled them deeper into the labyrinth of ancient trees, their path illuminated only by slivers of moonlight filtering through the dense canopy above.

The haunting echoes of the wolves' howls reverberated through the air, sending a chilling reminder of the danger that now lay behind them.

Branches reached out, grasping at their clothes, like skeletal fingers, threatening to ensnare them in the forest's treacherous embrace. Leaves rustled with a whispered warning, urging them to hasten their escape.

Shadows continued to dance around them, casting eerie silhouettes that seemed to mimic the wolves' predatory grace.

Fear propelled their feet faster, their breaths coming in ragged gasps. And then, as abruptly as it had begun, the chorus of howls ceased. Silence engulfed the forest, wrapping around them like a suffocating blanket.

Their footsteps faltered, the team coming to a breathless halt, their senses acutely attuned to the forest's ominous stillness. The absence of sound seemed to stretch into an eternity, punctuated only by the thumping of their hearts.

"Did we... lose them?" Holly's voice trembled with a mix of relief and lingering apprehension. "I think so..." Tico exclaimed, out of breath.

The team pressed on through the enchanted forest, their wary gazes scanning the treacherous undergrowth. The air crackled with an unsettling energy as if the very atmosphere itself warned of imminent danger. Twisted vines coiled like sinister tendrils while the eerie silence hung heavy, broken only by the occasional rustling of leaves and the whisper of the wind.

As they ventured deeper, the team began to notice a subtle shift in their surroundings. The air grew heavy with a pungent, musky scent, a telltale sign of danger that lurked nearby. Ava's intuition tingled, sensing a malevolent presence intertwined with the dark magic that plagued the forest.

Holly, her eyes wide with realization, pointed to the ground, her voice filled with trepidation. "Look! Viper prints… And they do not look like the normal coil-like ones a snake would usually make… I am sure these vipers have been touched by the dark magic. We need to be cautious."

The prints left by the vipers were sinuous and irregular, imprinted with an otherworldly aura that hinted at the corrupted power coursing through their veins. The team exchanged concerned glances, knowing they had to proceed with utmost care.

Suddenly, the underbrush erupted with a cacophony of hissing as a swarm of vipers slithered forth, their scales glistening with an unholy sheen. Their eyes, like molten rubies, held a hypnotic allure that threatened to ensnare the unwary.

Tico's voice rang out, his tone resolute. "Stay focused! Vipers usually have the ability to mesmerize their prey. But with the dark magic running in their veins, there is no telling what they are capable of. Keep your eyes locked on mine, and don't let their gaze bewitch you."

Ben stepped forward; his bravery undeterred by the formidable adversaries before him. "I'll distract them while you find a solution. Just be ready."

Holly, her mind racing with ideas, rummaged through her bag of supplies. Drawing on her knowledge of herbs, she swiftly mixed a concoction that counteracted the hallucinogenic effects of the vipers' venom. She handed the vial to the others, her voice steady but urgent. "Take this antidote. It should help you resist their illusions."

Ava, her telepathic abilities a valuable asset, communicated with Tico through their unspoken connection. "Tico, we need your agility. Find a rare herb called Moonleaf high in the trees. It will aid us in repelling the vipers."

Tico nodded, his muscles coiled with anticipation and deftly scaled the nearby trees. With uncanny precision, he collected the Moonleaf leaves, their silvery glow radiating an ethereal luminescence.

As the vipers closed in, their slithering forms becoming a menacing circle around Ben, the team sprang into action. Holly ignited a small fire, releasing the smoke from the Moonleaf leaves infused with the antidote. The thick haze billowed, forming a protective barrier that dispersed the vipers' enchanting illusions.

Ben, now shielded from the vipers' mesmerizing gaze, moved with lightning speed, evading their striking fangs with nimble agility. With each thrust of his blade, he fended off their venomous assaults, the clash of steel against scales reverberating through the air.

Ava, her telepathic link providing her with the vipers' intentions, directed her allies with unwavering focus. "Circle around, everyone! Keep them at bay while Ben holds them off."

The team formed a protective ring, their determined faces etched with resolve. With Tico's agility, Holly's knowledge of herbs, and Ava's telepathic guidance, they orchestrated a synchronized defense against the relentless vipers.

Bathed in the ethereal glow of the Moonleaf smoke, the team's movements became a dance of survival. They anticipated the vipers' strikes, countering with calculated precision. Each venomous fang that sought their flesh was met with swift parries and retaliatory blows.

As the vipers writhed in confusion, their enchanted power weakened, allowing the team to gradually gain the upper hand. They fought with unyielding fortitude, their hearts pounding in sync with the rhythm of battle.

Finally, the last of the vipers succumbed, retreating into the depths of the forest, their sinister presence vanquished by the team's resilience and resourcefulness. The air hung heavy with the scent of victory, mingling with the lingering echo of hissing whispers.

The team, their bodies still tingling with the adrenaline of their recent battle, took a moment to catch their breath and collect themselves. Beads of perspiration adorned their brows, glistening like tiny diamonds in the fading sunlight that filtered through the forest canopy.

Ava, her voice calm yet infused with lingering excitement, spoke first. "We did it, everyone. We faced the vipers head-on and emerged victorious. Let's take a moment to rest and recover."

They eased themselves onto a moss-covered log, the soft cushion providing a welcome respite for their weary limbs. The rhythmic sound of their breaths, harmonized with the gentle rustling of leaves, created a soothing symphony that echoed through the tranquil clearing.

Holly, her hands still trembling from the intensity of the encounter, took a deep breath, attempting to steady her nerves. She meticulously packed away her vials of antidote and herbs, ensuring each delicate container found its rightful place within her satchel.

Her movements were deliberate, yet her eyes revealed a mix of relief and lingering unease.

Ben, his muscles taut and poised for action, wiped the sweat from his brow with the back of his hand. He inspected his weapons with strict care, cleaning the blade that had repelled the vipers' venomous strikes. His gaze flickered to his companions, a silent acknowledgment of their shared accomplishment.

Tico, ever vigilant, scanned the surroundings, his sharp eyes darting from tree to tree. His hand instinctively reached for the hilt of his dagger, finding solace in the familiar weight against his side. He remained the protector, ever watchful, his senses attuned to any hint of danger that may lurk nearby.

As they dusted themselves off, the team exchanged glances, a silent understanding passing between them. The dark magic – wherever it was, did not want to be found and would do anything to keep them from finding it…

As dawn broke and the day began to mature, the team ventured deeper into the heart of the forest, their once serene surroundings metamorphosed into a tumultuous battleground, where nature waged a fierce war against their progress. The air crackled with an unsettling energy, a palpable manifestation of dark magic permeated the atmosphere. Ominous clouds loomed overhead, their brooding presence casting a foreboding shadow over the landscape as if warning the adventurers of the impending turmoil.

Suddenly, without a single forewarning, the tranquil ambiance completely shattered into disarray. A violent gust of wind tore through the forest, tearing at the trees and shrubs, its force augmented by the malevolent fragments of dark magic that swirled within its currents. The gusts howled with an otherworldly fury, a cacophony that drowned out any semblance of serenity. They whipped through the dense foliage, causing branches to writhe and leaves to spin in a frenzied dance of chaos.

The rain descended upon the team with a merciless intensity, each droplet a miniature torrent drumming against their weary bodies. The deluge pelted their backs, seeping through their clothing and chilling them to the bone. Their once-dry garments clung to their skin, laden with the weight of the storm's assault.

The once familiar paths that had guided them through the forest now appeared distorted and unfamiliar, morphed into twisted labyrinths by the dark magic's sinister influence. The enchanting allure of the woods had given way to an ominous haze of confusion, where every step became a gamble in an ever-shifting maze.

Holly, her trembling fingers clutching her soaked cloak tightly, struggled to find her footing amidst the relentless tempest. Each step she took sank her feet deeper into the mire of the muddy ground, threatening to ensnare her in its clammy grip. Her voice, barely a whisper amidst the roar of the storm, cracked with a mixture of fear and determination. "We... we need to find shelter!" she yelled; her words snatched away by the raging tempest before they could reach the ears of her companions.

Ben, usually determined in his bravery, squinted against the onslaught of rain, his steely gaze fixated on the obscured path ahead. His jaw clenched with an unyielding resolve, a defiance that refused to succumb to the storm's assault. "Stick close together!" he bellowed, his voice strained with a mix of urgency and determination. With outstretched arms, he reached for Ava's trembling hand, their fingers interlacing as if to anchor themselves to one another. "We can't let this storm get the best of us. We have to keep moving!"

Tico, his usual calm demeanor giving way to a furrowed brow, scanned their surroundings with an intensity born out of protective instincts. His eyes darted from one obscure figure to another, searching for any hint of danger within the maelstrom. "The storm is trying to confuse us, to make us lose our way," he warned, his voice strained with urgency, his words barely audible over the relentless cacophony. "We must trust our instincts and stay focused. Don't let the chaos cloud your minds!"

Battered by the unrelenting downpour, the team stumbled forward, their once agile movements reduced to a struggle against the elements. Each step felt like a battle, a desperate effort to remain upright against the onslaught of wind and rain. The howling gusts threatened to knock them off their feet, the wind's invisible hands pushing against their bodies with a rigid force. Raindrops obscured their vision, distorting the world into a blurry tapestry of shadows and cascading water.

Leaves and branches became frenetic dancers, swirling in a frenzy around the fraught team. The eerie vortex seemed to mock their efforts to escape, an ever-present reminder of their vulnerability amidst the whims of nature's wrath. The very fabric of the forest appeared to shift and rearrange itself, an illusion that toyed with their senses and led them astray with every desperate turn.

With every passing moment, the team's sense of despair grew, each rain-soaked breath weighed down by the oppressive atmosphere. Fear gnawed at their hearts, a relentless companion that threatened to overshadow their dwindling hope. The storm, with its fierce tenacity, seemed intent on crushing their spirits, breaking their resolve until all that remained was a hollow shell of defeat.

Yet, even as their energy flickered like a struggling flame, threatened to be extinguished by the overwhelming forces of nature, a tiny spark of resilience lingered deep within their souls. It whispered of the countless trials they had overcome; of the bonds they had forged in the face of adversity. It refused to be snuffed out, their persistence, a testament to the strength of their spirits.

In the midst of chaos, they clung to one another, their trembling hands interlacing, their bodies drawing closer for a semblance of comfort. Their bond became their anchor, the sole refuge amidst the tempest's fury. They fought against the storm's onslaught, their movements fueled by sheer willpower and a steadfast belief that they could overcome this trial.

Chapter Three

Ben and Ava clung to each other's hands; their fingers interlaced tightly as they battled against the storm's onslaught. The wind tore at their clothes, threatening to tear them apart. Rain lashed against their faces, stinging their skin with icy droplets. Panic welled inside them as they realized they had separated from Holly and Tico in the chaos.

Their calls for their friends were seized away by the howling winds, and their voices were lost in the tempest's wrath. Desperation etched across their features, they strained their ears, hoping to catch a faint sound, a response that would lead them back to safety. But all they heard was the ferocious symphony of the storm, a symphony that drowned out their pleas.

Blinded by rain and disoriented by the swirling foliage, Ben and Ava stumbled forward, their steps hesitant and fraught with uncertainty. The once familiar landmarks had disappeared, swallowed by the darkness and confusion. Trees loomed like spectral sentinels, their branches whipping with malevolent intent. Shadows danced and shifted in the flickering light, distorting reality, and playing tricks on their minds.

As they pressed on, their senses were assaulted by eerie sights and sounds. Whispering voices seemed to echo from all directions, their words twisted and distorted. Unsettling shadows writhed and warped, resembling abnormal forms that slithered through the undergrowth. The air itself carried a tangible malevolence, thick with the lingering presence of dark magic.

In the dim, hazy light, Ava's heart pounded against her chest as she glanced at Ben, her eyes wide with fear. "We... we have to find them," she managed to say, her voice quivering with uncertainty. "We can't... we can't be alone out here."

Ben's jaw clenched, a strong sense of purpose etched upon his face, even as worry knitted his brows. "We will find them, Ava," he vowed, his voice resolute. "We have to keep moving, keep searching. We can't let the storm tear us apart."

As they trudged forward, each step a treacherous endeavor, their eyes darted nervously through the enveloping darkness. Every rustle of leaves, every gust of wind, sent a shiver down their spines, the unseen specters of the forest lurking just beyond their line of sight. The storm seemed to conspire against them, its unrelenting fury sowing seeds of doubt and disarray.

Time lost its meaning as they stumbled through the deceitful terrain, their fear growing with each passing moment. They called out Holly's and Tico's names repeatedly, and their voices strained with a mixture of urgency and desperation. But the storm swallowed their words, leaving them feeling more isolated than ever.

Through the haze of rain and anguish, Ben caught a glimpse of a flickering light in the distance. Hope ignited within him as he tugged Ava's hand, pointing towards the elusive beacon. "Look, Ava! There!" he exclaimed; his voice filled with a glimmer of relief. "Maybe that's them! Let's hurry!"

With their bodies weary and their spirits battered, Ben and Ava stumbled upon the dilapidated remains of an old cottage hidden amidst the gnarled trees. The structure stood as a weathered testament to the ravages of time, its walls adorned with peeling paint and windows cracked like jagged veins. Yet, despite its outward appearance of abandonment, an unsettling aura of dark magic permeated the air, urging caution.

Casting a wary glance at each other, Ben and Ava exchanged silent reassurances before mustering the courage to step across the threshold. The creaking of the door echoed through the empty rooms as they cautiously entered, their eyes adjusting to the dimness within. The cottage's interior was shrouded in an eerie stillness, broken only by the flickering light of an ancient candle that danced upon a gnarled wooden table.

As their gaze swept the room, they caught sight of a hunched figure seated in the corner, her form obscured by tattered robes that clung to her like cobwebs. Clearly a witch, her withered visage was etched with countless lines, her eyes glinting with a malevolent gleam that sent a chill down their spines.

Ava and Ben cautiously approached the witch as she turned her gaze toward them, her piercing eyes seeming to hold a depth of knowledge beyond their comprehension. Her withered face softened, revealing a glimmer of curiosity. "What brings you to my humble abode?" she asked, her voice a mix of intrigue and suspicion.

Ava hesitated for a moment, her eyes meeting Ben's briefly before she mustered the courage to speak. "We were caught in the storm," she explained, her voice filled with genuine concern. "We got separated from our friends, and we don't know where they are."

Ben nodded; his voice calm yet tinged with worry. "We're lost. Would you be able to help us find them?"

The witch's gaze softened, her expression momentarily betraying a flicker of sympathy. "Lost in the storm, you say?" She stroked her chin, deep in thought. "The storm can be a treacherous ally, leading anyone astray. But fear not, for I may have a solution."

Ava's eyes brightened with hope. "Any assistance would be greatly appreciated."

The witch's lips curled into a knowing smile. "I possess a magic apple, imbued with the power to guide lost souls back to one another. If you consume it, its enchantment will lead you to your friends."

Ben's eyebrows furrowed slightly, a tinge of skepticism creeping into his voice. "An apple? Are you sure it's safe?"

The witch nodded; her voice laced with reassurance. "Rest assured, young ones. This apple is untouched by darkness. It will bring you back together with your friends, safe and sound."

Ava's curiosity got the better of her, and she tentatively reached out to accept the apple from the witch's outstretched hand. As her fingers grazed the apple's smooth skin, a jolt of energy coursed through her, making her recoil in surprise.

Ben's eyes widened, concern etching lines on his face. "Ava, are you alright?"

Ava took a deep breath, her voice trembling slightly. "I... I don't know. Something happened when I touched the apple. It was like a surge of power flowed through me..."

The witch's expression shifted, a glint of malice flashing in her eyes. "Ah, the consequences of meddling with forces beyond your understanding," she sneered. "For that, you shall pay the price."

Ava's voice quivered, her once confident tone now tinged with vulnerability. "I... I can't... My telepathic abilities they're gone. The witch stole them from me!"

Ben's eyes blazed with anger as he confronted the witch, his voice seething with accusation. "You deceived us, witch! You knew what would happen to Ava when she touched that apple, didn't you?"

The witch raised an eyebrow, her face a mask of innocence. "Deceived? I assure you, young man, I had no knowledge of the consequences. The apple was meant to guide you, not strip her of powers."

Ben scoffed; his voice laced with disbelief. "You expect us to believe that?"

The witch's voice turned sharp, her tone dripping with frustration. "I may wield magic, but I am not responsible for every twist and turn of fate. But since you deem me a traitor to the greater good, I have no choice but to show you the full wrath of magic I do possess."

No sooner had she uttered those words, her wicked presence began pulsating throughout the cottage. Shadows writhed and warped, walls shifting and morphing into a labyrinth of twisted corridors. The once familiar surroundings became a maze of deception, designed to trap, and disorientate.

Illusions danced before their eyes, tormenting their senses. The walls seemed to close in on them, their voices echoing in a cacophony of madness. Whispering voices filled the air, taunting them with cruel laughter and distorted warnings.

Ben's voice cut through the chaos, laced with resolve. "Don't be fooled by the illusions, Ava! We can't let fear cloud our judgment. This witch thrives on our desperation. We need to trust in ourselves and in each other. It's the only way we can withstand this twisted maze of dark magic!"

Their hearts pounded in sync as they navigated the twisting corridors, their steps measured and deliberate. The illusions grew more deceptive with each turn, the walls shifting and winding, leading them astray. Yet, Ben's resolve and Ava's resilience anchored them, their trust in one another, a guiding light in the darkness.

Through the ever-changing corridors, they encountered nightmarish scenes—an endless void that threatened to consume them, phantoms of their deepest fears that reached out with icy fingers.

As they fought through the labyrinth, their bond, and their trust in each other grew stronger. With every trap evaded, every illusion shattered, they defied the witch's expectations, unraveling her web of darkness.

Finally, as if the cottage itself recognized their willpower, the illusions dissipated, and the shifting walls solidified once more.

Ben and Ava cautiously moved toward the door of the decrepit cottage, their eyes fixed on the witch who stood before them, her expression a mix of fury and frustration. Rain dripped from the eaves, creating a melancholic melody that underscored the tension in the air.

With every step they took, the witch's snarls grew louder, her voice reverberating through the dilapidated walls. "You think you can escape me? You dare defy my magic?"

Ava's heart continued to pound in her chest as she cast one last glance at the witch, her features sick in a mixture of fear and determination. "We won't be prisoners to your darkness any longer," she declared, her voice steady despite the tremor in her limbs.

Ben's jaw set, his gaze locked eyes with the witch. "Your tricks won't hold us captive any longer. We're leaving, and you can't stop us."

As they pushed open the creaking door, a surge of adrenaline coursed through their veins. The storm outside raged on, rain cascading down in sheets, but the torrential downpour no longer felt as oppressive as the witch's presence within the cottage.

As they stepped onto the threshold, a burst of lightning illuminated the surrounding forest, casting an eerie glow on their escape. The air crackled with newfound energy as if the very elements were lending their support in their bid for freedom.

Ava glanced back, her eyes meeting the witch's enraged stare. The witch, now bereft of her ability to manipulate the cottage's interior, thrashed about in frustration, her spells futile against the strength of Ben and Ava's resolve.

With a defiant smile, Ava turned away, her voice carrying a note of triumph. "Your power ends here, witch. We will find a way to undo the damage you've caused."

The witch's furious cries echoed through the night, fading into the distance as Ben and Ava ventured further away from the cottage. They moved with purpose, their steps guided by a newfound purpose to reunite with Holly and Tico, to face the challenges ahead, and to restore Ava's lost abilities.

The rain continued to soak their clothes, the earth beneath their feet turning into a treacherous path of mud. Yet, each step they took felt lighter, as if the weight of the witch's influence had been lifted from their shoulders.

Ben and Ava stumbled through the dense thicket outside, their bodies trembling from the harrowing encounter with the witch. The storm raged on around them, rain pelting down in torrents and the air heavy with the scent of damp earth. Leaves and branches rustled under their frantic footsteps as they called out for their friends, their voices carried away by the howling wind.

"Holly! Tico!" Ben's voice carried through the storm, strained with desperation. "We're over here! Can you hear us?"

Ava's voice joined in, echoing through the thicket. "Please, we need you!"

Their calls seemed to hang in the air, carried by the wind and rain. For a moment, the forest remained eerily silent as if holding its breath. Then, a faint response reached their ears, a distant but unmistakable voice.

"Ben! Ava!" Holly's voice cut through the storm, filled with relief and urgency. "We hear you! Hold on! We're coming!"

With newfound hope, Ben and Ava followed the sound of their friends' voices, pushing through the thorny underbrush and tangled vines that seemed determined to impede their progress. The thicket swallowed their footsteps, and every step became a battle against nature's obstacles.

As they pressed forward, the storm began to relent, the rain easing to a gentle drizzle. The dense foliage above formed a makeshift canopy, offering a temporary respite from the continuous downpour. Light trickled through the canopy, casting ethereal rays that illuminated their path.

In the distance, Ben and Ava caught sight of two familiar figures emerging from the shadows—a disheveled but determined Holly, and Tico, their clothes drenched, and their faces etched with exhaustion. The reunion was bittersweet, their embrace was a mixture of relief and concern.

Holly's voice trembled with emotion as she held Ben and Ava tightly. "We were so worried! Are you both okay? What happened back there?"

Ava's voice wavered, her eyes glistening with unshed tears. "A witch... she took away my telepathic powers."

As the weight of their recent trials slowly ebbed away, Ben and Ava shared their harrowing experience with Holly and Tico.

"We were trapped in that cottage," Ben recounted, his voice still tinged with the adrenaline of their escape. "The witch, she had us under her spell, playing with our fears and trying to keep us captive. But we managed to break free."

Within a few minutes, the storm began to subside. The once turbulent atmosphere gave way to a gentle breeze that whispered through the trees, caressing the soaked leaves, and calming the restless forest. The clouds above started to disperse, revealing patches of clear sky where sunlight peeked through, casting a warm glow on the rain-soaked landscape.

Curious animals, sensing the shift in energy, cautiously emerged from their hiding places. Squirrels darted playfully among the branches, birds resumed their melodious songs, and rabbits hopped carefree in the undergrowth.

However, a few animals that had been affected by traces of the dark magic maintained a safe distance, their wary eyes fixed on Ben and Ava. They moved hesitantly; their movements stilted as if struggling against an invisible force. Some of them, fueled by residual aggression, attempted to attack but soon faltered, finding their strength diminished.

Ben observed the behavior of these affected animals, a mixture of sympathy and caution in his eyes. "The dark magic has left its mark on them," he murmured, his voice laced with a hint of sadness.

Ava extended her hand toward a skittish fox, its fur matted and its eyes flickering with fear and confusion. "It's okay," she whispered gently, her voice carrying a soothing melody. "We mean no harm."

The fox hesitated for a moment, its ears twitching in response to Ava's words. Slowly, it inched forward, sniffing the air, its once tense body relaxing. It seemed to recognize the truth in her words, finding comfort in the reassurance offered.

The forest around them seemed both welcoming and treacherous, for they had learned that even the faintest traces of dark magic could corrupt the creatures that inhabited these woods.

"We must proceed with caution," Ben warned, his voice tinged with a sense of urgency. "The residual dark magic may still affect the living things we encounter, but it is the deeper shadows we must be most wary of."

Holly nodded, her expression a mix of determination and concern. "We've seen how even a small amount of dark magic can twist and distort the creatures of the forest," she said. "But we can't let fear paralyze us."

Tico scanned their surroundings, his senses on high alert. "The presence of the lingering dark magic is very clear," he observed, his voice barely above a whisper. "But I sense a stronger concentration deeper within the forest. That's where the true danger lies."

Ava tightened the grip on her staff, her fingers tracing the intricate carvings etched into its surface. "We've come so far," she said, her voice filled with quiet resolve. "We can't turn back now."

With a collective nod, the group set off, their footsteps cautious yet determined. The forest responded to their presence, the rustling of leaves and the whisper of the wind carrying an unspoken promise of support.

CHAPTER FOUR

With the rain giving up its battle, the sky gave way to dusk, casting the entire forest in a soft hue of shadows. Ben, Holly, Ava, and Tico trudged through the muddied path, hoping to find a place to rest. Their clothes clung to their weary bodies, soaked through and heavy with dampness. Exhaustion etched deep lines on their faces, and weariness weighed heavily on their every step. The sound of their footsteps echoed through the mist-shrouded woods, a mournful rhythm that seemed to match their faltering spirits.

Holly's voice trembled with fatigue as she spoke up, "We can't keep going like this. We need to find somewhere to rest, even if it's just for a little while."

Tico's normally lively demeanor dampened by exhaustion added, "I agree with Holly. We can't push ourselves too hard. We need to regain our strength if we're going to face more challenges ahead."

On high alert, Ava cast a wary gaze around the eerie forest. The shadows moved with unsettling energy, and a chill ran down her spine. "I understand you're tired, but we can't afford to let our guard down. This forest is filled with dark magic and finding a safe resting place won't be easy."

Ben, his face etched with concern, spoke up. "Ava's right. We've already seen what this dark magic can do. We can't afford to take any unnecessary risks."

The group fell into a tense silence, the weight of their exhaustion and the lingering danger weighing heavily on their shoulders. Each of them knew the importance of finding shelter, but they also recognized the potential dangers that lurked within the forest's deceptive embrace.

As they deliberated, Ben, lost in his thoughts, failed to notice a fallen tree trunk obstructing his path. He stumbled over it, his ankle twisting painfully. A sharp cry escaped his lips as he crumpled to the ground, clutching his injured ankle.

"My ankle! I… I can't put any weight on it," Ben winced, his face contorted in pain.

Ava rushed to his side, and her worry etched on her face. "Ben, are you okay? Let me see."

Holly and Tico quickly joined them, their concern palpable. Holly's voice quivered with anxiety, "Oh no, Ben. This is terrible timing."

Tico knelt beside Ben, examining his ankle. "It looks like a sprain. We need to get you off your feet, find a safe place to rest, and tend to your injury."

Reluctantly, Ben nodded, realizing the urgency of their situation. "You're right. We can't stay out here in the open. We need shelter and a chance to recover. Let's find a place that doesn't have dark magic attached to it."

Ava, though still apprehensive, understood the necessity of their decision. She helped Ben to his feet, supporting him as they resumed their search for a suitable refuge.

The group moved cautiously; their progress hampered by Ben's injured ankle. They scanned their surroundings, seeking signs of a place untouched by the dark magic that permeated the forest. The wind rushed through the trees, carrying with it the faintest hints of hidden sanctuaries.

Suddenly, their eyes caught sight of a faint flickering light through the dense foliage. Intrigued and hopeful, they followed the glow, their footsteps guided by a glimmer of curiosity. The light led them to a secluded clearing, where a quaint wooden hut stood nestled amidst a tapestry of wildflowers and moss-covered stones.

The hut was adorned with delicate carvings of woodland creatures that seemed to come alive under the flickering lantern light. It exuded an air of magic and whimsy, yet its presence was shrouded in an aura of mystery. Smoke curled lazily from the chimney, mingling with the scent of damp earth, and freshly fallen raindrops.

Through the fogged windowpane, the group caught sight of figures within the hut. A lady with porcelain skin and cascading black hair moved gracefully, her ethereal presence illuminated by the warm glow of the hearth. She emanated an otherworldly radiance, her violet eyes filled with curiosity and caution.

Seven dwarves accompanied the lady, each bearing unique characteristics that made them easily distinguishable. Their weathered faces spoke of countless adventures, etched with lines of wisdom and tales untold. Their eyes darted between the approaching group and their mistress, their expressions filled with a mix of wariness and guarded curiosity.

As Ben, Holly, Ava, and Tico approached the door, the lady and the dwarves stood as a unified barrier, their eyes fixed on the weary travelers. The atmosphere was thick with doubt and apprehension, and a tangible tension hung in the air.

Ben cleared his throat, his voice laced with weariness and a touch of uncertainty. "Excuse us, but we've been caught in the storm, and... we were wondering if... if you might be able to offer us some shelter."

The lady's gaze flickered between the group, her eyes searching for signs of ill intent. Her voice, soft yet tinged with caution, broke the silence. "We have been alone in these woods for quite some time. Strangers are a rare sight. What brings you here?"

Holly, her voice gentle and sincere, stepped forward. "We mean you no harm. We are simply travelers seeking refuge from the storm. We're exhausted and long for a warm fire and a dry place to rest our weary bodies."

The eldest and most gruff of the group spoke up with a deep voice that resonated through the small space.

"We've been wary of strangers for good reason. This forest hides many secrets, and trust comes hard-earned."

Ava's eyes met the women's, and she detected a flicker of sympathy in her gaze. Ava's voice quivered slightly as she pleaded, "We're not here to cause trouble."

The dwarves continued to eye the weary travelers, their gaze lingering on the mud-soaked clothes and the exhaustion imprinted on their faces. The tension in the air seemed to amplify, the silence stretching into an almost unbearable weight.

Finally, the woman broke the silence, her voice carrying a gentle plea. "My name is Snowflake. This is Grumble, Swift, Glimmer, Puddle, Snicker, Bristle, and Whisker. And you are?"

As the group introduced themselves, the air seemed to clear itself of the uneasy tension.

"Let us give them shelter," Snowflake finally said as she glanced at the dwarves. "We cannot turn away those in need, especially on a night like this."

The little men exchanged one last look before nodding in unison, their suspicion easing slightly. With a hesitant yet welcoming gesture, Snowflake opened the door wider, inviting the weary travelers into the warmth of the hut.

"What happened?" Snowflake's voice was filled with genuine worry as she pointed to Ben's foot as he limped over the threshold.

Ava's voice tinged with relief, explained, "Ben tripped over a fallen tree trunk, and he hurt his ankle."

Snowflake's eyes softened with understanding as she gently placed a hand on Ben's shoulder. "Oh, dear! You've been through quite a trial. Let me help ease your pain."

Inside the hut, the air was filled with the soothing aroma of herbs and the crackling of a warm fire in the hearth. The walls bore elaborate carvings of woodland creatures, their forms etched with skill and precision. These intricate designs seemed to breathe life into the room, infusing it with an atmosphere of both comfort and enchantment.

Snowflake guided Ben to a comfortable chair by the hearth and gestured for the others to make themselves at home. She disappeared into a nearby room, returning with a basket filled with healing supplies and a soft cloth.

Sitting down beside Ben, Snowflake delicately removed his shoe and sock, revealing the swollen and tender ankle. Her gentle touch seemed to possess its own healing energy as she examined the injury with utmost care.

"Take a deep breath," Snowflake instructed, her voice laced with soothing reassurance. "I'm going to bandage your ankle and apply a warm compress to alleviate the pain and reduce the swelling."

As Snowflake worked, her hands moved with a graceful fluidity, skillfully wrapping a soft bandage around Ben's ankle. Her touch was comforting, and the warmth of her hands seemed to transfer soothing energy to the injured area.

Ben let out a sigh of relief, his tense muscles relaxing under Snowflake's attentive care. The pain gradually subsided, replaced by refreshing warmth that enveloped his ankle.

As Tico, Ava, and Holly settled into chairs by the hearth, the dwarves resumed their places around the sturdy wooden table. Their gazes still held a lingering wariness, but their actions spoke of a cautious acceptance. Snowflake moved gracefully, pouring steaming cups of herbal tea, and placing platters of warm food before the weary group.

The sound of the dwarves' hushed conversation filled the room. Whispers of concern and speculation mingled with occasional bursts of laughter as if they were testing the limits of their newfound trust.

Ava, her hands wrapped around the soothing warmth of the tea, mustered the courage to attempt conversation. "We're grateful for your kindness. We didn't expect to stumble upon such generosity in these treacherous woods."

Grumble, his voice gruff yet softened, responded, "You're the first visitors we've had in quite some time. We've grown accustomed to the solitude, but it's good to see new faces."

"Join us for a bite to eat," Snowflake gestured as the dwarves pushed extra chairs toward the table.

As the group settled into their seats at the dinner table, the atmosphere in the hut became infused with uneasy tension. Snowflake and the dwarves, seated around the sturdy wooden table, engaged in hushed conversation. During this moment, a heated argument erupted between Grumble and Snicker, their voices growing louder with each passing second.

Grumble, his gruff voice echoing through the room, pointed an accusing finger at Snicker. "I tell ya, Snicker, there's somethin' fishy about those peculiar footprints we found near the river! I reckon it's a sign of trouble."

Snicker, his eyes flashing with defiance, retorted, "Ah, don't be daft, Grumble! Those footprints were nothing but a prank by Puddle. You're just seeing shadows where there aren't any!"

Swift chimed in; his normally agile demeanor replaced by a solemn expression. "Calm down, you two! We've been through enough strife already. Let's not start quarreling amongst ourselves."

But Grumble, his patience wearing thin, slammed his fist on the table. "I'm tellin' ya, and we can't afford to ignore these oddities. Remember the time we dismissed that strange whisper in the wind, only to find ourselves knee-deep in trouble?"

Glimmer, his fair face pale and serious, interjected, "Grumble's got a point, Snicker. We can't dismiss every oddity as a prank. There's something in these woods; we'd be fools to think we're immune."

Puddle, who had been sitting slouched in his chair, listening quietly, suddenly straightened up. His voice, usually filled with joviality, carried a somber tone. "I don't like all this talk. It gives me the creeps; it does. We've got to stick together and keep our wits about us."

The argument seemed to reach a stalemate as the dwarves fell silent, their gazes shifting uncomfortably between each other.

Holly glanced around a sense of foreboding tightening her chest. She noticed a subtle change in the demeanor of Snowflake and the three dwarves closest to her.

Snowflake's porcelain features, once radiant and serene, now bore a distant and almost vacant expression. Her violet eyes, which had sparkled with warmth, now seemed dull and detached. She moved mechanically, her graceful gestures lacking the usual fluidity and grace. Snowflake's behavior seemed detached from the joyful atmosphere that had permeated the hut just moments before.

To Holly's right, Swift, who she found to be nimble and filled with restless energy, sat with a peculiar stillness. A distant gaze replaced his usual wide-eyed curiosity, his attention seemingly focused on something far beyond the confines of the hut. He appeared to be lost in his own thoughts, oblivious to the conversations around him.

With his radiant smile and lighthearted presence, Glimmer wore a solemn expression. His fair complexion, once shimmering with an inner glow, now appeared pallid and lifeless. His voice, usually filled with lightness and laughter, was absent from the jovial banter that echoed through the room. Glimmer seemed to withdraw into himself as if an invisible weight rested upon his shoulders.

Puddle, a jolly prankster, sat slouched in his chair, his usually round belly now sunken and his rosy cheeks drained of color. An unsettling silence replaced the hearty laughter that had once filled the room. Once sparkling with mischief, Puddle's eyes stared blankly into the distance, devoid of their usual mischievous twinkle.

Sensing the unsettling atmosphere, Ava exchanged a concerned glance with Ben and Tico. The three of them observed the strange behavior of Snowflake and the three dwarves, trying to make sense of the disquieting shift. They exchanged whispers, their voices hushed with unease.

Ben leaned toward Ava and whispered, "Something isn't right. It's as if Snowflake and the dwarves are distant, disconnected from the joy and warmth that surrounded us moments ago. I can't shake this sense of darkness."

Ava nodded, her voice barely above a whisper. "I noticed it too. It's almost as if their spirits have been dimmed, like shadows lingering in the corners of their beings. We need to be cautious."

Holly's gaze shifted to Snowflake, who sat at the head of the table, her eyes fixed on her plate, seemingly lost in her own thoughts. Holly mustered the courage to break the uneasy silence, and her voice tinged with concern. "Snowflake, is everything alright? You seem... distant."

Snowflake's response was a faint murmur, her voice distant and devoid of its usual warmth. "I'm fine. Just lost in my thoughts, I suppose. Please, enjoy your meal."

The rest of the dwarves appeared oblivious to the strange behavior, engaging in lively conversation and hearty laughter. Their voices mingled with the clinking of silverware and the crackling of the fire, starkly contrasting the unease that hung in the air.

As the strange behavior of Snowflake and the dwarves cast a shadow of unease over the dinner table, the adventurers exchanged worried glances. Ben, Ava, Holly, and Tico sensed that something was amiss, and their suspicions grew that the same dark magic they had encountered in the town before, and the forest had infiltrated the very walls of the hut. They knew they had to investigate discreetly without drawing the attention of the unsuspecting dwarves and Snowflake.

With silent determination, Ben signaled to his companions, motioning for them to follow his lead. They excused themselves from the table, one by one, claiming a need to freshen up or stretch their legs. As they dispersed, they reconvened in a corner of the hut, huddled together, their voices hushed but urgent.

Ava leaned in; her eyes filled with concern. "We can't ignore this anymore. It's clear that the strange behavior of Snowflake and the dwarves is tied to the dark magic we encountered in Perlitan and in the forest. We need to find out what's causing it."

Holly nodded, her expression reflecting the gravity of the situation. "Agreed. But we must be careful. We don't want to alert Snowflake or the dwarves. Let's search for clues quietly."

Tico glanced around, ensuring that no one was within earshot, before chiming in. "I noticed a small storage room near the back of the hut. It might be a good place to start. We should look for anything out of the ordinary."

With their plan in place, the adventurers discreetly made their way to the storage room, stepping lightly to avoid drawing attention. The room was dimly lit, filled with shelves of supplies and various odds and ends. Their eyes scanned the room, vigilant for any remnants of the dark magic that had haunted them during their journey.

Ben's sharp gaze caught a glimmer on the floor near one of the shelves. He knelt, his fingers brushing against the smooth surface. "Look," he whispered, his voice barely audible. "Black residue. It could be remnants of the magic that has lost its power."

Ava crouched beside him, studying the residue intently. "It seems to have lost its potency, but it's a clear sign that this hut has been touched by dark magic."

They moved methodically, scanning each shelf, and inspecting every nook and cranny. Their search was both urgent and delicate, as they didn't want to raise suspicion among the dwarves or Snowflake. Each item they touched was examined for any hint of residual magic, any trace that could unravel the mystery before them.

Ben's voice was low but filled with conviction as he addressed the group. "It's clear that Snowflake and the dwarves have been in contact with the same dark magic that left Perlitan and that has now plagued the forest. We need to keep a close eye on them and observe their behavior for any signs of the magic's influence."

Ava nodded in agreement, and her eyes focused on the affected individuals. "We need to determine the extent of their involvement. Are they aware of their actions, or are they mere puppets under the magic's control?"

Holly's gaze shifted between the dwarves and Snowflake, her mind processing the information they had gathered. "We should pay attention to any unusual or out-of-character behavior. Changes in their demeanor, speech, or actions could be indicative of the dark magic's influence."

Preparing themselves for a longer stay with their new friends, Tico, Ava, Ben, and Holly made their way back to the table, trying hard not to let their thoughts cloud their judgment.

Chapter Five

As next day began and the time came for Ben, Holly, Ava, and Tico to bid farewell to Snowflake and the seven dwarves, a bittersweet heaviness settled over their hearts. They knew their true mission had just begun, and they had to uncover the truth behind the dark magic that had affected half of the dwarves. But they also had to be cautious and protect themselves from the potential dangers that lay ahead.

Standing outside the quaint wooden hut, bathed in the soft glow of twilight, Ben, Holly, Tico, and Ava exchanged glances, their eyes reflecting a mixture of determination and concern. Snowflake and the dwarves, oblivious to their true intentions, bid them farewell with warm smiles and heartfelt gratitude.

Snowflake, her porcelain features now tinged with a hint of sadness, addressed the group, her voice soft and filled with melancholy. "It was a pleasure having you as our guests."

Ava stepped forward; her voice steady but laced with underlying suspicion. "Thank you, Snowflake. We are truly grateful for your hospitality and the kindness you've shown us."

Ben, Holly, Ava, and Tico reciprocated the farewells, their voices sincere, but their minds focused on the hidden truth.

They continued to wave until the hut and its inhabitants faded from view, their figures melding into the dense forest backdrop.

Once the hut was out of sight, the group halted, their eyes scanning the surroundings for any signs of prying eyes. Only when they were sure they were safe from detection did they gather in a small clearing, hidden from prying eyes and nestled within the embrace of towering trees.

Ben, his voice calm but filled with grit, broke the silence. "Now, we must be careful. We cannot let anyone discover our true purpose."

Ava, Tico, and Holly nodded in agreement, their eyes scanning the area for any signs of movement.

With their plan set, they emerged from the clearing. Their movements were stealthy, blending seamlessly into the natural rhythm of the forest. They weaved through the underbrush, their senses sharp, ever watchful for any signs of danger.

Hiding in the bushes, the group observed as the dwarves readied their tools, preparing for their journey to the mine. The atmosphere was thick with suspicion, a cloak of uncertainty shrouding their every move.

Tico whispered, his voice barely audible, "We must follow them, but we must exercise the utmost caution to avoid detection. We need to know what's really happening in that mine."

Ava nodded, her eyes never leaving the dwarves. "Agreed. We need uncover the truth, but we must also protect ourselves. This dark magic is powerful and dangerous. We can't afford to underestimate its reach."

Ben's gaze flickered between Snowflake and the dwarves; his voice tinged with concern. "And keep a close eye on Snowflake too. If she's involved, we need to know the extent of her role."

Her voice filled with determination, and Holly whispered, "Let's be patient and observant. We need concrete evidence before we act. The lives of those in the mine depend on our prudence."

The tension in the air was palpable as the dwarves began their march, their steps determined and resolute. Snowflake, graceful and ethereal, walked beside them, her presence an enigmatic juxtaposition to the suspicion gnawing at the group.

Ben, Ava, Holly, and Tico stealthily trailed behind; their steps carefully placed to minimize any noise. They moved from one hiding spot to another, blending into the natural cover of the forest like phantoms observing the land's secrets. Their hearts raced with anticipation and unease as they followed the dwarves deeper into the woods, their eyes trained on every movement and interaction.

Whispers of conversation drifted through the air, snippets of dialogue that heightened their suspicion. The dwarves discussed the mining operation, the tools they needed, and the route they would take. Snowflake's voice, distant and detached contributed little to the conversation, her thoughts seemingly lost in a haze.

As the group weaved through the dense forest, Ben, Ava, Tico, and Holly couldn't shake the nagging feeling that something was profoundly amiss. The dwarves' behavior, their urgency to reach the mine, and the eerie detachment of Snowflake fueled their growing suspicions.

Ava, her voice barely above a whisper, broke the silence. "We're drawing closer. Stay vigilant but be careful not to reveal our presence. The answers we seek lie ahead."

The group nodded in agreement; their eyes focused on the dwarves who were now within reach. The sound of pickaxes clinking and boots trudging through the underbrush grew louder with each passing moment, echoing like a haunting symphony of labor.

As Grumble, Snicker, Whisker, and Bristle entered the mouth of the mine, their figures disappearing into the darkness, a heavy silence settled over the secluded clearing. Swift, Glimmer, Puddle, and Snowflake lingered outside, their sinister expressions revealing a hidden darkness that had taken hold of them. The atmosphere was ominous and thick with despair, the weight of their actions hanging heavily in the air.

Ben, Ava, Holly, and Tico, concealed among the trees, watched with growing horror as Snowflake and the affected dwarves made their way to a secluded clearing beside the mine. Their steps were purposeful, their movements cold and detached. The group could hardly believe their eyes as they witnessed the unfolding scene.

In the clearing, four cages stood side by side, each one containing a human captive. Their once- vibrant spirits dimmed; the prisoners were haggard and withered, their faces etched with fear and desperation. The sight of them sent a chill down Ava's spine, and her heart sank with a mixture of sorrow and anger.

In the first cage, a middle-aged man with disheveled hair and dirt-streaked skin slumped against the iron bars. His eyes once filled with vitality, now reflected a mixture of exhaustion and anguish. His calloused hands, once strong and capable, trembled with weariness. Deep lines etched his face, telling stories of hardship and struggle. Tattered clothes hung loosely on his thin frame, a stark contrast to the sinewy strength that remained. His voice, hoarse from crying out, pleaded intermittently for freedom and mercy.

Beside him, a young woman huddled in the second cage, her once-flowing locks now matted and unkempt. Tear stains marked her dirt-smudged cheeks, highlighting her hauntingly beautiful features. Her eyes, once bright with hope, now glistened with despair. Her delicate hands clutched the bars, fingers trembling with fear and uncertainty. The remnants of a torn dress clung to her skeletal form, a painful reminder of her lost dignity. She rocked back and forth, her movements an expression of her shattered spirit.

In the third cage, an elderly man sat with stooped shoulders, his weathered face lined with a lifetime of toil. His weary eyes held a flicker of defiance, a testament to the resilience within him. Gnarled from years of labor, his trembling hands clutched a tattered blanket that offered little comfort against the biting cold. His voice, weakened by years of hardship, whispered words of solace to his fellow captives, instilling hope in the darkest of moments.

In the last cage, a young boy with tousled hair and tear-streaked cheeks sat huddled, his tiny frame lost in the shadows. His wide, innocent eyes searched the clearing for any sign of salvation but only found the cold, indifferent gaze of the dwarves. His small fingers clutched a worn-out teddy bear, its worn patches a testament to the years of companionship it had provided. He trembled from fear and the biting chill of captivity, his voice quivering as he softly whimpered for his mother.

These captives, once strangers, now bound together by shared suffering, emanated an aura of desperation. Their faces bore the marks of physical and emotional torment, etching a heartbreaking narrative of lives robbed of freedom. They exchanged glances filled with silent solidarity, their eyes revealing stories of loss, resilience, and an unwavering will to survive.

Their spirits, though battered, were not entirely broken. Each captive, in their own way, clung to the flickering ember of hope, nurturing it against the suffocating darkness. Their desperate nature reflected their yearning for liberation, their firm belief that there must be a way to escape this cruel fate.

Ben's voice quivered with disbelief, his words barely escaping his lips. "This can't be happening. The dwarves... Snowflake... they've been capturing innocent people and subjecting them to this misery."

Ava, her eyes filled with tears, clenched her fists in frustration. "How could they? We trusted them and believed in their kindness. We were guests in their home, and they betrayed us and these poor souls."

Her voice trembling with anger and despair, Holly whispered, "We must help them. We can't stand idly by and watch this unfold. These innocent lives depend on us."

Tico, his voice filled with determination, responded, "We will help them, Holly. But we must gather more information and understand the full extent of Snowflake and the dwarves' plan. We need solid evidence to expose their darkness."

The group huddled closer together, their eyes fixed on Snowflake and the dwarves.

Snowflake's porcelain features, now tinged with an eerie paleness, stood tall amidst the captives, her presence both ethereal and foreboding. Her icy blue eyes, once warm and inviting, now gleamed with an unsettling intensity. Her now silver-white hair cascaded down her slender frame, its lustrous strands contrasting sharply with her now-pallid complexion. Her delicate fingers, adorned with ornate rings, curled around a staff that crackled with dark energy.

Beside Snowflake stood Swift, a dwarf whose features were marred by a sinister twist. His weathered face bore deep lines, marking the toll of time and the weight of his actions. His once- sparkling eyes now held a dullness, and their vibrancy was lost to the darkness that had consumed him. His stout frame, adorned in worn-out leather armor, emanated a menacing aura as he clutched a whip tightly in his calloused hands.

Glimmer wore a twisted grin upon his fair face. His golden curls, usually bouncing with delight, now seemed lifeless, as if drained of their former vibrancy. His eyes, once filled with mischievous glimmers, were now hollow, their light extinguished. His slender figure, adorned in tattered robes, appeared gaunt, a mere shadow of the festive spirit he had once been.

Puddle sported a mocking sneer that marred his otherwise jovial expression. His plump cheeks, usually rosy with laughter, now sagged with an air of malevolence. His round eyes, once filled with mirth, now held a malevolent gleam, their mischievous spark twisted into a chilling gaze. His stout figure, clad in garments of dark hues, exuded a sense of eerie authority as he stood with crossed arms.

Once filled with warmth and kindness, Snowflake's voice reverberated through the dimly lit chamber, carrying an unsettling weight. "Work diligently, my captives. Your labor is essential to our grand design. We need every ounce of precious ore extracted from this mine."

Swift, his voice laced with a cold resolve, stepped forward. "Remember, any sign of defiance or rebellion will be met with swift punishment. You exist solely to serve our purpose, toiling until there's nothing left in you."

Glimmer, his fair face twisted with malice, chimed in. "And let's not forget the magic that keeps you compliant. Resist, and you shall suffer the consequences. We can't have any disruptions or escapes."

His tone dripping with hatred, Puddle added, "Indeed, we've done quite well so far, haven't we? Your labor is worth its weight in gold and will serve our purpose. Your lives are insignificant compared to the power we seek."

Snowflake's voice, cold and distant, filled the chamber. "Remember, this is all for the greater cause. Our power will grow, and our dominion will expand. We stand on the precipice of greatness, and you are the steppingstones to our ascent."

The captives, their faces fixed with weariness and fear, listened to the dwarves' instructions with a mixture of resignation and defiance. Their gazes flickered between Snowflake and the affected dwarves, searching for any shred of humanity, any hint of mercy, but finding none. The weight of their situation pressed heavily upon their shoulders, and they could only pray for a glimmer of hope amidst the darkness that enveloped them.

Snowflake added. "Make sure they work tirelessly, Swift. We need to extract every bit of precious ore from this mine. Our power demands it."

Swift nodded obediently. "Don't worry, Snowflake. We'll ensure they work until their last breath. Their labor will serve our purpose."

The group watched in silence, their hearts heavy with hopelessness and anger, as Snowflake and the dwarves approached the cages. The captives trembled in fear, their eyes pleading for mercy.

One captive, a young woman with tear-streaked cheeks, pleaded desperately for her life. "Please, let me go! I have a family, children who depend on me. Have mercy!"

Snowflake's voice, devoid of compassion, cut through the gloom. "Your pleas are meaningless. You are mere pawns in a grand design, and your purpose will be fulfilled."

The affected dwarves stood by their expressions cold and indifferent, as the captives were forced into the mine and instructed to prepare for a hard day of work. The group, hidden among the shadows, witnessed the harsh treatment, the whip-like commands, and the dehumanizing conditions imposed upon the captives.

As they moved silently through the dimly lit tunnels, the horrified group took in the scene before them. The captives labored relentlessly, their bodies weary and broken, their spirits barely flickering. The walls of the mine glistened with the remnants of precious ore; a stark reminder of the value placed upon the suffering of others.

Whispers of agony and anguish filled the air, mingling with the sound of clinking chains and the heavy thud of tools against the rock. Each step the group took brought them closer to the captives, their hearts heavy with the weight of their desperation.

Snowflake's voice reverberated through the tunnels, her words cutting through the oppressive atmosphere. "You're nothing more than tools in our grand design. Your lives mean nothing compared to the power we seek."

One captive, his voice filled with defiance, cried out, "You can't do this! We are not your slaves! We deserve freedom!"

The dwarves, their expressions hardened, sneered at the captive's pleas. "Freedom is a luxury you cannot afford. Your purpose is to serve and serve you shall."

Tico, Ava, Ben, and Holly moved silently through the mine, their hearts heavy, and their minds consumed by the need for justice.

The low-hanging chamber within the mine, adorned with glistening rocks and flickering torches, loomed before the captives as they were forcefully thrust into the laborious task of excavating.

The captives, sweat-soaked, swung their tools with a determined fervor. The sound of metal against rock filled the chamber, echoing off the walls like a desperate plea for freedom. Their fatigued bodies yearned for respite, but there was no rest to be had, for the gaze of the dwarves and Snowflake lingered upon them.

Ben, his voice barely a whisper, interjected amidst the sounds of labor. "We must uncover the truth, but we cannot act rashly. We need to find the other dwarves and understand their role in this. They might hold the key to understanding the extent of Snowflake's darkness."

Holly, her brow furrowed with concern, replied, "But what if they are already aware, complicit in this cruel scheme? Or worse, what if they are also under the influence of dark magic? We can't assume they will be our allies."

Tico, his gaze hardened, added, "Regardless of their knowledge or involvement, we won't find answers if we don't confront them. We need their insight, and if they are not aware, we can expose the truth and rally their support against Snowflake."

Ava, her fortitude fixed, shook her head. "If we want to get to the bottom of this and save everyone involved, we must join forces with the other dwarves. Together, we stand a better chance of unraveling the darkness and putting an end to this treachery."

Ben's voice, filled with quiet grit. "We'll need to bide our time and choose the right moment to make our move. We can't afford to alert Snowflake and the affected dwarves."

With their resolve strengthened, Ben, Ava, Holly, and Tico watched in silent anguish as Snowflake and the dwarves led the captives deeper into the mine, disappearing into the darkness. Their path was treacherous, but they were determined to bring an end to the nefarious plot and restore hope to those whose lives had been shattered.

CHAPTER SIX

In the heart of the daunting mine, the captives worked relentlessly, their once-vibrant spirits subdued by the crushing weight of their labor. The air hung heavy with the scent of sweat and minerals, while the deafening echoes of pickaxes striking rock reverberated through the cavernous space, amplifying the sense of despair that permeated the atmosphere.

Amid this grim scene, Ben, Holly, Ava, and Tico stood together, their faces a blend of concern and determination. Shining with a glimmer of hope, their eyes were fixed on a daring plan that would lead them to the truth behind the dark magic ensnaring their companions.

As the sun dipped below the horizon, its final rays painted the mine with an amber glow, casting long, haunting shadows on the worn faces of the captives. The adventurers silently observed the unaffected dwarves, now their only hope to break the curse of dark enchantment plaguing their friends. Swift, with his piercing eyes; Glimmer, emanating an ethereal aura; Puddle, whose solemn gaze hinted at hidden depths; and Snowflake, whose cold demeanor concealed secrets they desperately sought to unveil, all stood watchful guard over their fellow dwarves, making every step towards them a perilous endeavor.

Not to be deterred, Ben, with his agile mind, conceived a diversion that would momentarily distract the watchful guardians. He skillfully loosened a support beam at the mine's entrance, cunningly orchestrating a controlled collapse of rocks. The tremors jolted the affected dwarves and Snowflake into action, and they rushed to assess the potential danger.

In the ensuing chaos, like shadows in the twilight, Ben, Holly, Ava, and Tico slipped away, the flickering light from their torches illuminating their path as they ventured deeper into the mine's labyrinthine passages. Each twist and turn revealed a new facet of the mine's mysterious charm – stalactites and stalagmites adorned the cavern's ceiling and floor, dripping with crystalline water that glimmered like stars in the night sky. The earthy scent of minerals mingled with the dampness, and the sound of dripping water formed an eerie symphony that echoed through the dimly lit tunnels.

At last, they discovered a secluded chamber, a secret haven hidden away from prying eyes. Its walls, adorned with a mesmerizing array of glowing crystals, cast an otherworldly luminescence that bathed the room in a captivating glow, giving it an aura of enchantment and mystique.

As they approached the resting unaffected dwarves – Grumble, his weathered features etched with years of wisdom and strength, Snicker, whose perpetual grin seemed to conceal both humor and sorrow; Whisker, whose bushy beard seemed to absorb the light around him; and Bristle, whose stern gaze conveyed a sense of responsibility – Ben initiated the conversation with hushed reverence. The adventurers' words seemed to blend with the essence of the chamber, carrying the weight of their quest for the truth.

"We need to talk," Ben began, his voice a mere whisper. "We believe that dark magic is affecting our friends. Can you help us understand what's happening?"

The unaffected dwarves exchanged puzzled glances; their expressions uncertain as they grappled with the possibility of an unseen menace within their midst. Grumble, the eldest of the group, spoke first, his voice resonating with wisdom, tinged with a hint of trepidation. "Dark magic? We don't know what 'ya talking about. We ain't noticed anything out of the ordinary."

With her gentle yet inquisitive demeanor, Holly probed further, her eyes seeking the truth buried beneath the surface. "Are you absolutely certain? Think carefully. Have you encountered anything unusual or experienced memory lapses?"

Whisker scratched his head thoughtfully, his furrowed brow evidence of the earnest contemplation taking place. "Now that you mention it, there have been moments when certain details seemed to evade our memory, like pieces of a jigsaw puzzle missing from the whole."

His eyes bright with newfound insight, Tico chimed in, "That's it! It's not that you've turned a blind eye; the dark magic is causing selective amnesia, stealing precious fragments of your experiences!"

Ava nodded in agreement, her features mirroring the unwavering purpose that marked her character. "We need to find a way to help you remember. Perhaps if you write down your experiences as they unfold, you might retain a firmer grasp on the truth."

The unaffected dwarves exchanged glances, uncertainty mingling with their desire to aid their afflicted friends. Finally, Grumble spoke with a fresh resolve, "We'll give it a shot. But only for the next two days."

Thus, over the next two days, the adventurers remained close to the unaffected dwarves, providing encouragement and guidance as they diligently documented their experiences in worn, weathered notebooks. Yet, despite their collective efforts, the notes remained tinged with uncertainty, and the memories they sought to reclaim seemed elusive, slipping through their fingers like grains of sand through an hourglass.

On the appointed day, the group reconvened in the depths of a dense forest, nature's embrace providing a semblance of comfort amidst the looming uncertainty. The unaffected dwarves, their eyes gleaming with a mixture of anticipation and concern, presented their meticulously written notes – an intricate tapestry of ink-stained parchment bearing the burden of forgotten truths.

"We saw Snowflake and the others leading the captives into the mine," Grumble read aloud, his voice tinged with gravity. "But we ain't know anything about the reason behind their actions."

Snicker added, his grin fading into a solemn expression, "Sometimes, we catch fleeting glimpses of something peculiar, shimmering around them like a mirage that defies focus."

Bristle, his demeanor one of steadfast resolve, chimed in, "We tried to reason with them, but they appear... different, as if their very essence has been altered."

Tico leaned forward, his eyes ablaze with understanding, "As we suspected, the dark magic is manipulating their hearts and minds, turning them into unwitting agents of malevolence. They are unwittingly aiding in the extraction of the ore, all while entrapped by the curse's insidious influence."

In the dimly lit forest clearing, Grumble, Snicker, Whisker, and Bristle stood huddled together with Ben, Ava, Holly, and Tico, agreeing to assist in freeing their friends. The air was thick with a mix of anxiety, desperation, and confusion as they grappled with the weight of their solemn task.

The towering trees loomed over them, their gnarled branches casting intricate patterns of shadows on the ground below, where vibrant wildflowers bloomed amid the fallen leaves.

Grumble exuded an aura of seasoned concern as he spoke first, his voice rumbling like distant thunder.

"Aye, we can try talking to them, reasoning with them. Perhaps they may awaken from this malevolent trance if we can illuminate the dark magic's deceptive grip on their minds."

Snicker stroked his bushy beard while interjecting with a dash of cynicism, "But let's not forget, we've tried that before. Their hearts seem locked in stubborn resistance, unwilling to hear any rational argument."

Whisker scanned the clearing's perimeter, his sharp eyes darting from shadow to shadow. "Attempting to break the dark magic's grasp on them is an option, but we must tread carefully. The risk of inadvertently causing harm to both our friends and us is a lurking possibility we cannot dismiss."

Bristle spoke softly, "Maybe our quest should be to discover a way to counter the dark magic's evil effects, to shield them from harm while liberating them from its wicked sway."

Their whispers ebbed and flowed like a gentle breeze rustling through the leaves, the natural world bearing witness to their deliberations. The moonlight filtered through the canopy above, creating a mystical ambiance as it bathed the clearing in its eerie glow.

Ava's eyes shimmered with empathy, her voice tender and soothing, "We cannot risk causing harm to those we cherish, but neither can we stand idle as they inflict pain on others. There must be a middle ground to break the dark magic's chains without resorting to violence."

Holly shared her insights, "Perhaps we could embark on a quest to unearth a counter-spell or a mystical artifact capable of nullifying the malice that entwines them. It shall be a formidable journey, but the prospect of liberating our dear friends is worth every effort."

Tico added his astute observations, "If we wish to thwart this dark magic, we must first study their behavior closely. Every step and gesture might unveil a pattern or vulnerability we can exploit to gently break their shackles."

Grumble's brow furrowed, his mind an intricate web of strategies and concerns. "In our pursuit of liberation, we must approach with caution. One misstep and the consequences could be dire. The line we walk is perilously thin."

Snicker nodded, his quick wit as sharp as the edge of a finely crafted blade, "And let's not forget, once they discover our intentions, they'll unleash a torrent of fury upon us. We must have a contingency plan, an escape route if all else fails."

Whisker let out a sigh, the gravity of their quest palpable in the air, "Our hearts ache at the thought of facing our cherished friends in battle. Nevertheless, we must stand firm, for we cannot allow them to bring harm to innocent souls."

Bristle's eyes brimmed with unshed tears, "Perhaps we can create a diversion, a clever ruse to draw them away from those they hold captive. When they're distracted, we may have an opportunity to break the dark magic's hold."

The dwarves fell into a contemplative silence, the cool night air enveloping them like a comforting embrace. The chirping of crickets and the distant hoot of an owl served as a haunting backdrop to their thoughts, echoing the gravity of their chosen path.

Finally, Ben stepped forward, his resolute stance emanating steadfast fortitude, "We need to study the dark magic, searching for chinks in its armor and avenues of liberation. And if, by all misfortune, all our efforts fail, we must be prepared to face our friends, not with swords drawn, but with hearts heavy and sorrowful."

A somber yet resolute air settled over them as their decision took root in the forest clearing. The moonlight danced among the leaves, painting shifting patterns on the ground as though nature shared in their anticipation of the trials ahead. With determination etched upon their faces, the brave adventurers set forth on their journey to confront the dark magic and, ultimately, save their cherished companions from the clutches of malevolence.

As the following evening descended in with a hushed stillness as the last rays of the setting sun painted the sky with a tapestry of warm colors. The dwarves and their companions found themselves nestled in a quaint wooden hut tucked away amidst the forest's ancient trees. As they gathered around a rough-hewn table, the comforting scent of hearty stew and freshly baked bread wafted through the air, enticing both stomachs and hearts.

The hearth crackled and popped, its dancing flames casting playful shadows on the hut's walls. The warm glow illuminated the room, revealing the cozy furnishings adorned with handcrafted tapestries and intricate wooden carvings depicting scenes of folklore and adventure. The soft glow highlighted the camaraderie that incased the room as laughter and lighthearted banter danced through the air like fireflies on a summer's eve.

But amid the apparent mirth and friendship, an underlying tension couldn't be ignored. The unaffected dwarves, Grumble, Snicker, Whisker, and Bristle were masters of concealing their intentions, their weathered faces revealing nothing of the gravity that weighed on their hearts. They exchanged furtive glances as they observed their friends, the affected dwarves and Snowflake, who seemed to bear the brunt of an invisible burden.

Snowflake, usually a vision of otherworldly grace, appeared diminished, her once vibrant aura now dulled by the oppressive weight of the dark magic that ensnared her. Like the petals of a snow- white lily, her alabaster skin was tinged with a pallor that betrayed her exhaustion. Her normally shimmering eyes now held a haze of confusion and weariness.

As she took a deep breath, the air around her seemed to hold its breath in unison, and for a fleeting moment, a spark of clarity shimmered in her violet eyes. The others watched silently, hoping to catch any information thread that might lead them to a solution.

"I... I can feel the struggle," Snowflake's voice was a fragile whisper that carried a world of pain. "The dark magic's influence is relentless, and I... I can't fight it on my own."

The gravity of her words hung heavily in the air, like the thick fog that sometimes encircled the forest. Each word seemed to be woven with the threads of sorrow and desperation, tugging at the heartstrings of those who listened.

The other affected dwarves nodded in agreement; their usually lively spirits subdued briefly as they wrestled with the dark magic's grip on their souls. Their expressions mirrored a silent plea for salvation, a desperate hope that they might return to themselves once more.

Grumble exchanged a subtle glance with the other unaffected dwarves, a wordless acknowledgment passing between them that they needed to tread carefully. These fleeting moments of clarity were their only windows into the souls of their friends, and they needed to seize them to glean any information that could aid their quest to save them.

The thoughtful and gentle Whisker spoke up, his voice a soothing balm amid the storm of emotions. "Snowflake, is there anything you can remember? Any detail about the dark magic's origin or how it found its way into the hut?"

Snowflake's brow furrowed; her delicate features creased with the effort of trying to grasp elusive memories. "I... I remember the darkness creeping in slowly, like a shroud covering everything in its path," she began, her voice tinged with anguish. "It felt...

irresistible, like a promise of power and control. But now... now it feels like a nightmare I can't escape."

Snicker interjected with a glimmer of hope, "And when did it start? Was there anything different that day, any event, or visitor that might have triggered this?"

Snowflake shook her head, her eyes brimming with frustration at her inability to recall the critical details. "I... I can't remember. It's all so foggy, like trying to grasp a wisp of smoke. But it's been days, maybe even longer, and it's been spreading, consuming everything in its wake."

Bristle leaned in closer to Snowflake, offering a gentle touch on her shoulder. "We'll find a way to help you, Snowflake. We won't let this darkness consume you or our friends."

Snowflake's gaze met Bristle's, gratitude and fear intertwining in her eyes like a dance of moonlight on water. "Thank you," she whispered. "I don't know what I'd do without you all."

The unaffected dwarves exchanged glances, a silent understanding passing between them. Their hearts were heavy with the weight of their burden, but they knew they had to remain steadfast and united to face the challenges that lay ahead.

As the night wore on, the hut seemed to cocoon them in its protective embrace. The soft glow of the hearth and the gentle crackling of the fire provided a sense of comfort amidst the uncertainty. Outside, the ancient trees stood as silent witnesses to the unfolding events, their gnarled branches casting eerie silhouettes on the forest floor.

As the moon rose in the star-studded sky, its silvery light spilled through the window, painting luminescence patterns on the wooden walls. The creatures of the night joined in a symphony of chirps and calls, adding an otherworldly chorus to the night's atmosphere.

Later that evening, under the moon's watchful gaze, the unaffected dwarves carefully slipped out of the hut, their steps as quiet as the whispers of the breeze through the leaves. The Enchanted Forest welcomed them in its mystical embrace, a tapestry of moss-covered trees and luminescent flowers unfolding around them.

The shadows danced and swayed as the adventurers made their way to the prearranged meeting spot, where Ben, Holly, Ava, and Tico waited, hidden in the cloak of darkness. The forest seemed to hold its breath as if nature sensed their quest's urgency.

The group gathered in a small clearing, the moonlight casting a silver veil over their faces. Their expressions were a mosaic of determination, fear, and hope, like constellations painting the night sky. Grumble took a deep breath, his voice carrying the weight of responsibility.

"We managed to get some valuable information from Snowflake and the other dwarves," he began, his words like lanterns illuminating the darkness around them. "The dark magic's hold is relentless, and Snowflake is struggling to resist it. We must act quickly."

Ava nodded, her emerald eyes reflecting her undaunted purpose. "We need to find a way to break the dark magic's influence, but we have to be cautious. We can't risk endangering them or ourselves."

Tico added, "We should try to find the source of the dark magic, its origin. If we can cut it off at its roots, maybe we can weaken its hold."

Soft yet filled with conviction, Holly's voice floated on the night breeze, "And we must find a way to restore their memories, to help them remember who they are and what they stand for."

Together, the adventurers and unaffected dwarves agreed that their missions would be split in two: Grumble, Bristle, Whisker and Snicker would stay behind, keep an eye on Snowflake and the affected dwarves while finding a way to release the captives. Ben, Holly, Ava and Tico had the job of exploring the dark magic while testing theories on how to disperse the evil darkness.

The forest seemed to echo their intentions, the rustling leaves, and the soft sigh of the wind a testament to the grave task at hand. In a circle bound by solemn resolve, they pledged to break the malevolent hold of dark magic that gripped their friends turned family. Faces etched with determination, they stood united against the encroaching shadows, their collective strength poised to reclaim those ensnared by the sinister forces they defiantly opposed. With a shared vow echoing through the air, they readied themselves for the trials ahead, a steadfast alliance against the looming darkness.

chapter seven

The night hung heavy with anticipation as the unaffected dwarves, Whisker, Bristle, Grumble, and Snicker, prepared for their next mission. In the dim light of their makeshift camp, nestled within the protective embrace of the Enchanted Forest, they meticulously checked their gear and whispered strategies under the watchful gaze of the moon.

Grumble, his aged face etched with wisdom, double-checked the bindings of his trusty pickaxe, the weight of their mission pressing heavily on his broad shoulders. "We cannot afford to fail," he murmured to the others, his voice a low rumble.

Whisker, his sharp eyes scanning the forest's perimeter for any signs of danger, nodded in agreement. "Aye, we must free the captives before the dark magic tightens its grip further. Every moment counts."

Bristle, his expression one of quiet contemplation, adjusted the straps of his satchel, ensuring that their supplies were secure. "And we must keep a close eye on Snowflake and the affected dwarves. They may pose a threat, but they are still our kin."

Snicker, ever the voice of reason tinged with cynicism, scoffed softly. "Bah, those lads and lasses don't know their own names, let alone pose a threat. But we'll keep an eye on 'em, just in case."

With their preparations complete, the unaffected dwarves set off into the forest, their footsteps muffled by the thick carpet of fallen leaves. Each step brought them closer to their destination – the hidden encampment where the captives were held prisoner by the dark magic's sinister grasp.

Grumble surveyed the scene with a practiced eye, his mind already formulating a plan of action. "We must act swiftly and with precision," he declared, his voice a command that brooked no argument. "Whisker, Bristle, Snicker – you take the eastern cages. I'll handle the ones to the west."

The unaffected dwarves nodded in silent agreement, their determination shining bright in the moonlight as they approached their assigned tasks with the precision of expert miners.

As Grumble and Snicker unlocked the cages containing the captives, a mix of relief and confusion adorned the faces of the once-imprisoned villagers. Whisker and Bristle approached the captives, their expressions blending empathy with steadfast resolve.

Whisker extended a steady hand to the nearest dwarf, his eyes conveying understanding. "Fear not, friends. We've come to free you from this dark enchantment."

The middle-aged man, still disoriented from their ordeal, looked up with a mix of gratitude and suspicion. "Who are you? Why are you helping us?" he stammered.

Bristle, his tone reassuring, responded, "We're your allies, untouched by the dark magic. Our mission is to break this curse that has befallen our kin. We need your help to return safely to the village."

Another captive, a young woman with worry etched on her face, cautiously approached Grumble. "But what about Snowflake? She seemed so... lost."

Grumble's eyes softened, and he nodded in understanding. "Aye, Snowflake is under the sway of the dark magic. We aim to find a way to help her, but first, we must get all of you to safety."

As the cages opened, the captives began to emerge tentatively, their limbs stiff from confinement and their minds still clouded by residual darkness. Whisker offered words of encouragement to each one, his voice a soothing balm amid the chaos.

"Take your time," he advised, helping a captive regain their balance. "The effects of the magic will fade, and you'll find your clarity once more."

Meanwhile, Bristle engaged in conversation with the elderly man, his gaze sincere. "We understand this must be bewildering but trust us. We've faced cursed lands before, and together, we can overcome it."

Snicker, with his typical dry humor, chimed in, "Don't worry, folks. The worst is behind you. Soon, you can now run back to the warmth of the village get a comforting meal and go wash away these dark memories."

As the captives started to regain their composure, whispers of gratitude and uncertainty filled the air. The unaffected dwarves continued their careful dialogue, offering assurances and guidance to ease the villagers' transition from captivity to liberation.

But their moment of triumph was short-lived as Snowflake and the affected dwarves appeared on the scene, their eyes blazing with fury and confusion.

Blinded by the spell that ensnared her, Snowflake raised her hands, conjuring a wall of frozen ice to stop the captives from making it back to the village, simultaneously a barrage of ice shards spiraled through the air like deadly projectiles headed in the direction of the unaffected dwarfs.

"Stop them!" she cried, her voice a chilling echo that reverberated through the clearing. "Do not let them escape!"

The unaffected dwarves knew they had to act quickly to disarm the affected dwarves and calm Snowflake before things escalated further. With practiced precision, they pushed the affected dwarves into one of the cages, locking the door securely behind them to prevent any further interference.

Snowflake's rage knew no bounds as she unleashed a torrent of icy fury upon the unaffected dwarves, her powers fueled by the dark magic's malevolent influence. But with quick reflexes and a steady hand, Grumble and Snicker managed to pull Whisker and Bristle out of harm's way just as the frozen shards threatened to engulf them.

As the ice wall around them began to melt under the warmth of the rising sun, the captives seized their chance to escape, making a run for it toward the safety of the nearby town. The unaffected dwarves watched with bated breath, their hearts pounding in their chests as they wished for their friends' safety.

But their moment of relief was cut short as Snowflake turned her attention back to them, her eyes glazed over with the dark magic's influence. The unaffected dwarves knew they had to act quickly to calm Snowflake down before she could cause any further harm.

"Listen to our voices," Grumble pleaded, his tone a mixture of desperation and purpose. "Focus on us, not the darkness that clouds your minds."

For a fleeting moment, Snowflake seemed to waver, her eyes clearing as she struggled to resist the dark magic's hold. But their victory was brief as the darkness once again enveloped her, dragging Snowflake back into its sinister embrace.

As the unaffected dwarves concentrated on dealing with Snowflake, they momentarily overlooked the captive affected dwarves. Seizing a sudden burst of erratic energy, the affected dwarves broke free from their confinement, adding a layer of complexity to the situation.

Just as the affected dwarfs and Snowflake were on the brink of unleashing what appeared to be a surge of dark magic and power upon the unaffected dwarfs, an unseen force seemed to seize control of them. In a sudden and unexpected reversal, they snapped up, their actions shifting as if guided by a different source, and they promptly began to retreat. It was as if an external influence had momentarily interrupted their hostile intentions, leaving the unaffected dwarfs both relieved and puzzled by this sudden change in behavior.

As Snowflake and the affected dwarves retreated back to their hut, their minds lost to the darkness, the unaffected dwarves breathed a sigh of relief, knowing that they had narrowly averted disaster. But their thoughts quickly turned to the captives and the tale they would tell the townsfolk when they returned home.

"We may have saved them for now," Whisker mused, his voice tinged with uncertainty, "but what will they say when they return to town? How will they explain what happened here tonight?"

Bristle shook his head, his brow furrowed with worry. "Only time will tell," he replied, his voice heavy with resignation. "But for now, all we can do is hope that they find a way to make sense of this madness."

With heavy hearts and a sense of urgency, the unaffected dwarves trailed behind Snowflake and the affected dwarves as they made their way through the dense undergrowth of the Enchanted

Forest. Every step felt like a weight upon their shoulders, their minds filled with worry and apprehension.

Snowflake, her once graceful stride now faltering, led the way with the affected dwarves in tow. Their movements were erratic, their eyes clouded with confusion and despair. The unaffected dwarves exchanged worried glances, silently communicating their shared purpose to keep a close watch on their friends, hoping that their volatile emotions wouldn't flare up again.

As they journeyed deeper into the forest, the air grew thick with tension, the slightest rustle of leaves sending shivers down their spines. They moved with cautious determination, their senses alert for any signs of trouble.

At last, they reached the entrance to the dwarves' home, a cozy cavern nestled within the roots of an ancient tree. Snowflake hesitated for a moment before disappearing inside, the affected dwarves following behind her like shadows in the darkness.

The unaffected dwarves exchanged a knowing look before cautiously venturing inside, their footsteps echoing softly against the cavern walls. They moved with silent precision, keeping a safe distance from their friends while remaining vigilant for any signs of danger. Amidst the tension, the unaffected dwarfs couldn't help but notice the familiar routine their friends, Snowflake, and the other dwarves, were suddenly back to doing, adding an extra layer of intrigue to the mysterious happenings.

Inside the cavern, the air was heavy with the oppressive weight of the dark magic, its malevolent presence palpable in every shadowy corner. Snowflake and the affected dwarves moved about with an air of resignation, their movements mechanical and devoid of emotion.

The unaffected dwarves watched from the shadows, their hearts heavy with sorrow as they witnessed the toll the dark magic was taking on their friends. They knew they had to tread carefully, their every move calculated to avoid triggering another outburst of volatile emotions.

CHAPTER EIGHT

Sitting around the fire in a clearing on the other side of the forest, Ben, Holly, Ava, and Tico discussed their next steps, their voices hushed with anticipation and uncertainty. Ben leaned forward, his expression pensive.

Ben, the adept leader of the group, grew up in a village of arcane mysteries, where his sharp intellect and innate magical affinity made him a natural leader. Renowned for his wit and an exceptional ability to solve puzzles and perceive hidden connections, Ben's high IQ and mastery of magic set him apart. A voracious reader of ancient texts, he effortlessly guided his companions through the most perplexing challenges, establishing himself as an indispensable leader among adventurers.

"You know," Ben began, "there's an ancient library, Sorcerous Archives, rumored to hold knowledge about magic, its origins, and how to wield it. It's said to be a repository of centuries- old wisdom, hidden away from the world."

Ava's eyes brightened with interest. "The library you're talking about, it's not just any library. It's a treasure trove of arcane knowledge, a place where magic secrets have been preserved through the ages."

Ava, resolute and knowledgeable, boasts a deep understanding of magic and alchemy, inherited from a lineage immersed in the arcane. Her childhood, surrounded by ancient tomes and bubbling potions, laid the foundation for her formidable skills. Renowned for her expertise, Ava's sharp mind and proficiency in the mystical arts make her an invaluable companion, fostering trust among fellow adventurers who rely on her unparalleled knowledge.

Holly, her gaze distant as she imagined the possibilities, added, "Legends say that this library contains volumes upon volumes of texts, scrolls, and tomes, each containing insights into various aspects of magic. If we want to understand the dark magic affecting Snowflake and the dwarves, this could be our best chance."

Despite being the youngest, Holly, a magical historian, honed her expertise amid ancient tomes and aromatic herb gardens. Nurtured in a home where history and herbal healing converged, she emerged as a sought-after scholar. Holly's distinctive fusion of botanical and archival knowledge created an enchanting tapestry that seamlessly linked the past, present, and future.

Always quick to strategize, Tico chimed in, "It could be the key to unraveling the mysteries of the dark magic, finding its source, and discovering a way to counter its influence. If there's any place that holds the answers we need, it's this ancient library."

Tico, the group's vigilant protector and skilled fighter, hails from an elf-like family deeply connected to the earth. Raised with a balance of strength and intelligence, his agile and brave nature makes him an unwavering guardian. Intrigued by magic and enchanted artifacts from a young age, Tico's dual prowess in combat and mysticism establishes him as a valuable asset, ensuring the safety of the group with his watchful dedication.

Ben nodded; his eyes determined. "I agree. We need to investigate this library. It's located deep within the heart of the enchanted forest, hidden from those who seek to misuse its knowledge. The journey won't be easy, and we'll face challenges along the way, but the rewards could be invaluable."

Ava leaned closer to the fire, the flames glowing warmly on her features. "But the library's history is shrouded in mystique. It's said to have been established by the ancient world's most skilled and wise magicians. They gathered their knowledge, spells, and discoveries and safeguarded it all in one place, a sanctuary of wisdom."

Holly's eyes sparkled with excitement as she added, "It's an incredible plan, but even getting into the library won't be easy. The keepers are whispered to be magnificent magical beings."

The group exchanged knowing glances as the fire crackled and the night breeze rustled through the trees. They understood the significance of their decision. The ancient library held the potential to be their guiding light in the darkness that had taken hold of their friends. With that, the decision was made, and their path was set.

As morning draped the forest in its gentle glow, the dwarves prepared to return to the hut. There, they would keep a watchful eye on Snowflake and the affected dwarves. Meanwhile, the adventurers embarked on their journey through towering mountains and vast fields, navigating dense forests and crossing meandering rivers along their path.

The mountains stood like ancient sentinels, their craggy peaks reaching for the sky. Jagged rocks and boulders lined the paths, a testament to the rugged terrain they traversed. Fields stretched endlessly, a patchwork of wildflowers and tall grasses swaying in the breeze.

After hours of trekking, they stumbled upon a small village nestled amidst the ancient trees, its rustic cottages and winding pathways hidden from view until they were nearly upon it. Smoke rose lazily from chimneys, and the sound of laughter and chatter drifted through the air, giving the impression of a tranquil haven untouched by time.

Approaching cautiously, the adventurers noticed that the villagers regarded them with a mixture of curiosity and wariness, their gazes lingering on the strangers who had ventured into their midst. Sensing the need to gain their trust, the adventurers sought out the town elder, a wise figure rumored to hold the secrets of the village.

The elder, a respected figure with a wrinkled face and eyes that gleamed with hidden knowledge, greeted them with a leisurely nod. "Welcome, travelers," he said, his voice carrying the weight of years. "What brings you to our humble village?"

Ava stepped forward, her demeanor respectful yet resolute. "We seek passage to the ancient library," she explained, her words carefully chosen. "We've heard whispers of its existence, and we believe it may hold the answers we seek."

The elder regarded them thoughtfully, his gaze piercing yet unreadable. "The library is indeed a place of great power and wisdom," he acknowledged. "But gaining access is no simple task. It requires trust, and trust must be earned."

With that, he set them a challenge: to prove their worthiness by aiding the villagers in a time of need. Only then would he reveal the location of the library and grant them passage.

The town elder's challenge for the adventurers is to aid the villagers in protecting their harvest from a sudden infestation of magical pests that threaten to decimate their crops. With the livelihood of the village hanging in the balance, the adventurers are called upon to prove their worthiness by facing this unexpected trial.

As the adventurers survey the fields, they are met with chaos. Swarms of shimmering insects, their wings aglow with magical energy, descend upon the crops, devouring everything in their path. The villagers work tirelessly to fend off the pests, but their efforts seem futile against the relentless onslaught.

Determined to aid the villagers and demonstrate their capabilities, the adventurers spring into action. With Ava's keen understanding of magical creatures, Ben's strength, Holly's resourcefulness, and Tico's agility, they devise a plan to repel the pests and save the harvest. Drawing upon their collective skills and knowledge, they set about implementing traps, barriers, and magical wards to protect the crops, they also empower the villagers with knowledge and skills to defend against future threats.

Ava takes charge, using her telepathic abilities not only to guide the insects away from the fields but also to teach a group of villagers how to communicate with and redirect the creatures in the future. Ben, recognizing the importance of long-term defense, collaborates with village elders to fortify the defenses, imparting his knowledge of strategic planning and stonework so that they can continue to strengthen the village's protections.

Meanwhile, Holly's resourcefulness shines as she shares her expertise in potion-making and spell craft with interested villagers, showing them how to concoct repellents and protective charms to safeguard their crops. Tico, with his agility and skill in combat, not only drives away the pests but also trains a group of villagers in basic combat techniques, ensuring that they are prepared to defend their land should similar threats arise in the future. As the sun begins to set, the tide of battle turns in favor of the adventurers and the villagers. The pests, unable to withstand the combined efforts of the adventurers, retreat into the depths of the forest, leaving the crops unharmed.

With the crisis averted, the adventurers return to the village center, where they are greeted as heroes by the grateful villagers. The town elder, his eyes filled with pride, acknowledges their bravery and resourcefulness.

"You have proven yourselves worthy," he declares, his voice ringing with admiration. "But remember, the library holds challenges far greater than any you have faced. Only by working together and trusting in each other can you hope to succeed."

He then offers them a map, intricately drawn with paths through the dense forest. "Follow this map," he instructs, "and it will lead you to the entrance of the library. But remember, the journey ahead will not be easy. The library holds secrets that only those who prove themselves worthy may uncover."

With a final nod of encouragement, the elder bids the adventurers farewell, his words lingering in their minds as they set out on the next leg of their journey.

As they neared the site marked on the map, the tales collected during their travels heightened their sense of hope, weaving a narrative that hinted at the possibility that this was the legendary place they had heard so much about. Finally, they arrived at a building that seemed to emerge from the very heart of the forest—an ancient library, its existence confirmed by the markings on the map. Their hearts quickened with excitement as they realized the truth: they had found the fabled library they had been seeking all along.

The library was a structure of weathered stone, its walls covered in intricate carvings that depicted scenes of magic, wisdom, and the passage of time. Ancient trees surrounded the building, their crooked branches reaching out as if to welcome the adventurers, while birds chirped melodiously from their perches.

However, their excitement was short-lived as they realized the library's entrance was barred. A heavy stone door stood between them and the repository of knowledge they so desperately sought. Ben's brow furrowed as he examined the door, his eyes narrowing in contemplation.

"It seems we've reached another obstacle," he mused aloud, his voice carrying a mix of resolve and frustration.

Ava's gaze swept over the door's intricate carvings, her mind racing. "Perhaps there's a way to unlock it, a hidden mechanism or a key we need to find."

Holly's fingers traced the edges of the carvings as she muttered, "Or maybe it requires something more than physical means. Perhaps a riddle, a test of our wit."

Tico leaned against the doorframe; his arms crossed. "Whatever it is, we need to solve it if we're going to gain entry to the library. Let's take a moment to think this through."

Their hushed conversation was interrupted by a soft rumbling sound. The ground beneath them vibrated slightly, and the door itself seemed to shift, revealing a small opening that hadn't been there before.

Ava's eyes widened as she realized what was happening. "Look, the door is opening! It's as if the library is inviting us in."

Stepping inside, they found themselves in a chamber bathed in soft, golden light. The air was thick with the scent of ancient parchment. In the center of the room stood a pedestal, upon which rested a single, ancient tome.

The tome emitted a faint glow as they approached the pedestal. Upon its cover was a riddle intricately engraved in a familiar and foreign language.

Holly read the riddle aloud, her voice echoing in the chamber. "In shadow and light, we weave our tales of mysteries, secrets, and paths that never fail. Speak my name, and I shall guide you to the wisdom within these walls."

The group shared glances, faces marked by a mix of curiosity and resolve as they contemplated the mysterious riddle laid out before them.

Ben's brow furrowed as he pondered. "It's a puzzle about names and stories. Perhaps we need to figure out the name of something related to the library."

Contemplating the riddle, Tico, utilizing his keen investigative prowess, deduced, "It must be Ink; they use it to craft stories and navigate the intricate tapestry of mysteries."

The erroneous response reverberated through the ancient chamber, causing tremors that echoed like disapproval from the very stone beneath their feet. A network of cracks swiftly crawled across the mystical walls, and an ominous rumble filled the air, foretelling the fragility of their once- sturdy sanctuary. Unfazed, the adventurers braced themselves for a second attempt, recognizing that the enigmatic forces dwelling within required a more precise and respectful answer.

Anxiety tinged with resilience, Ben drew upon a tale shared by a local, remembering the name of the ancient guardian of the library. "Echo, it has to be Echo watching over this place," he mused, the insight dawning upon him.

With a second misinterpretation, the room convulsed more intensely, revealing the perilous consequences of their errors. Dust and ancient debris cascaded from the ornate ceiling, casting an ominous haze. Anxiety set in as the very essence of the chamber seemed to reject their misjudgments. Bracing for the final attempt, the adventurers felt the weight of the guardian's displeasure.

Ava's eyes lit up as a realization dawned on her. "Wait, the answer might be 'books.' They're what hold the stories, the wisdom, the mysteries."

Holly's face brightened with excitement. "And books are what weave tales in shadow and light, capturing the essence of knowledge. 'Books' is the answer!"

As the word left her lips, the room's quivering ceased, the mystical foundations steadied, and a collective breath released into the still air. The tome on the pedestal emitted a soft hum. Its pages began to turn on their own, revealing intricate illustrations and ancient text. The room filled with warm, inviting light, and the door to the heart of the library swung open.

Inside the library, the adventurers found themselves in a realm of enchantment and knowledge that exceeded their wildest expectations. The magical ancient library, concealed behind a seemingly ordinary façade, expanded into a sprawling realm of endless shelves and winding passages within.

The library seemed like the perfect place where the art of architecture and the pursuit of wisdom intertwined seamlessly. Intricately enchanted, it harnessed mystical forces to defy the limitations of space, creating a vast expanse within its confines that far surpassed the modest exterior.

Tall, ornate bookshelves lined the walls, stretching upward to meet the vaulted ceiling adorned with intricate murals that depicted scenes of magic and enlightenment. The shelves themselves were masterpieces of craftsmanship, their dark wood intricately carved with patterns and motifs that whispered of centuries of study and contemplation.

The library's design invoked a sense of sacredness as if they were entering a sanctuary dedicated to pursuing higher understanding. Rays of sunlight filtered through stained glass windows, casting a kaleidoscope of colors across the polished floors and the dusty tomes that called the library home. The air was tinged with the aroma of aged parchment, a fragrance that spoke of countless stories and the passage of time.

The room was a symphony of silence, broken only by the faint rustle of pages as scholars and seekers of knowledge moved through the aisles, absorbed in their studies. The adventurers wandered among the shelves; their footsteps muffled by the plush carpets that lined the floor. They ran their fingers along the spines of ancient books, their leather covers worn smooth by the touch of countless hands.

As they explored, they discovered hidden alcoves and reading nooks, each offering a quiet haven for those who sought solace in the written word. Elaborate desks and plush chairs stood ready to cradle the curious minds of scholars while ornate ladders leaned against the towering shelves, allowing access to even the most elusive tomes.

The atmosphere was one of reverence and awe, where the mysteries of the universe seemed to dance between the pages of each book, waiting to be unraveled by those who dared to seek them. The library was a labyrinth of knowledge, a repository of ancient wisdom that held the potential to illuminate the darkest corners of their quest.

With each step they took, the adventurers felt the weight of history and magic enveloping them, drawing them further into the heart of the library's secrets. It was a place where time itself seemed to stand still, where the boundaries between reality and imagination blurred, and where the answers to their questions might lie hidden, waiting to be discovered in the hushed whispers of the pages.

As they ventured deeper into the library's depths, their excitement mingled with a sense of reverence. They were ready to embark on a journey of discovery, to uncover the truths that could save their friends from the clutches of dark magic. And in the embrace of the library's timeless knowledge, they knew that every step forward was a step toward unraveling the mysteries that had brought them to this enchanted place.

With a sense of purpose, the group moved through the labyrinthine aisles of the library. They were on a quest to find the section of the library that housed information about dark magic, hoping to uncover clues that would aid them in their mission to save Snowflake and the affected dwarves.

Ava's heart weighed heavy with the burden of her lost telekinetic abilities. She couldn't shake the lingering sadness that clouded her thoughts, uncertain of how to broach the subject with her companions. With each passing moment, the weight of her silence grew heavier, casting a shadow over their quest.

She traced her fingers along the weathered spines, lost in thought as she wrestled with her inner turmoil.

As they walked, their eyes wandered over the countless shelves, each filled with volumes that held secrets and knowledge spanning the ages. The library has a section dedicated to every conceivable magic and arcane wisdom branch.

Holly paused by a shelf adorned with books on elemental magic, her fingers tracing the titles. "It's incredible how much knowledge is housed here. From elemental magic to ancient incantations, it's like a treasure trove of arcane wisdom."

Ava nodded in agreement, her gaze sweeping over the shelves that held volumes of herbalism and alchemy. "And look at this collection on herbal remedies and alchemical transformations. It's fascinating how magic is intertwined with the natural world." Her thoughts briefly wandered to her mother, a skilled healer who had disappeared under mysterious circumstances. Ava's dedication to mastering the arcane arts was driven by a desire to uncover the truth about her mother's fate and to honor her legacy.

Tico's eyes sparkled as he perused a section dedicated to mystical creatures. "I've always been fascinated by creatures like griffins and phoenixes. It's amazing to think that people have dedicated their lives to studying them."

Ben, his expression determined, interjected, "As fascinating as all this is, we're here for a reason. We need to find the section that deals with dark magic."

Ben, ever perceptive to Ava's moods, approached her with a gentle touch on her shoulder. "Are you alright, Ava?" he asked softly, his concern evident in his voice.

Ava sighed, her gaze fixed on the floor as she struggled to find the words. "I... I miss my telekinetic abilities," she admitted, her voice barely above a whisper. "I feel... incomplete without them."

Ben's expression softened with empathy, a silent understanding passing between them. "I know it's been tough, Ava," he replied, his voice filled with reassurance. "But we'll find a way to help you get them back. I believe in you."

A flicker of hope ignited within Ava's heart at Ben's words, bolstered by the unwavering support of her friend. With renewed determination, she resolved to search the library for answers, determined to reclaim what she had lost.

Their steps quickened as they continued to explore the library, guided by their shared goal. They passed by sections on ancient spells, divination, and enchantments, each section more intriguing than the last.

Holly glanced at a shelf full of volumes of curses and hexes, a shiver running down her spine. "Curses have always been a double-edged sword in magic. They can hold immense power but also have great responsibility."

Tico's gaze lingered on a section dedicated to magical artifacts, his eyes lighting up. "Imagine the stories behind these artifacts. They've witnessed centuries of history and magic."

As they delved deeper into the library's hidden chambers, Ava's intuition guided her to a secluded alcove tucked away amidst towering shelves of ancient texts. There, she stumbled upon a weathered tome, its pages yellowed with age and adorned with intricate runes.

"This could be it," Ava whispered, her voice trembling with anticipation as she flipped through the pages, her eyes alight with newfound hope.

Ben peered over her shoulder, his curiosity piqued. "What is it?" he asked, his voice tinged with excitement.

"It's a ritual," Ava replied, her fingers tracing the faded text with reverence. "A ritual for restoring lost magical abilities."

A surge of hope coursed through them both as Ava began to decipher the ancient incantations and gestures detailed within the tome. With each word spoken, each motion performed, the arcane energies of the library responded, weaving a tapestry of magic that enveloped Ava in its embrace.

Ben watched in awe as Ava's resolve fueled the ritual, her connection to the magic growing stronger with each passing moment. And then, in a moment of radiant brilliance, Ava's telekinetic abilities returned to her, her power restored in full force.

Tears of joy welled in Ava's eyes as she realized the magnitude of what she had accomplished. She turned to Ben, her voice filled with gratitude. "Thank you,

Ben," she said, her words a heartfelt expression of their unbreakable bond. "I couldn't have done it without you."

Ben smiled, his own eyes shining with pride. "You never lost faith, Ava," he replied, his voice filled with admiration. "And now, you're stronger than ever."

With Ava's telekinetic abilities restored, she was now ready to face whatever challenges lay ahead in their quest for knowledge and enlightenment.

Ava's voice, now infused with excitement and urgency, echoed through the library's ancient halls as she feverishly scanned the titles on a nearby shelf, her eyes darting from one faded spine to the next in search of sections devoted to dark magic.

"We need to focus," she exclaimed, her tone filled with a sense of urgency. "Snowflake and the dwarves are in danger, and we can't afford to get lost in the wonders of the library."

Ben's eyes were fixed on the books before them, his voice firm. "You're right, Ava. Let's keep moving and find the section we're looking for."

As they moved deeper into the library, their determination only grew stronger. Each passing moment reminded them of the urgency of their mission. They knew that the key to saving their friends lay hidden within the pages of the books they sought.

Ben's voice broke the silence, his words laced with determination. "We're getting closer. I can sense it. We need to find the section on dark magic and see if there's any information that can help us."

Holly's brows furrowed as she scanned the shelves, her concern evident. "I just hope we're not too late. Snowflake and the dwarves are depending on us."

Ava's hand gently rested on Ben's arm as they continued their search. "We'll find what we need, Ben. We won't let our friends down."

Amid the towering shelves, Ben's eyes lit up as he spotted a section of books with foreboding titles and ominous covers. He pointed excitedly, his voice calm but filled with triumph, "There it is! The dark magic section."

Ava's face mirrored his enthusiasm as she replied, her excitement was palpable, "Finally, we're getting somewhere. Let's gather as much information as we can."

Holly's fingers gently traced the spines of the books, her voice tinged with anticipation, "These books hold the key to understanding the dark magic that has ensnared Snowflake and the dwarves. Let's start our research."

Tico's gaze swept over the shelves, his eyes alight with curiosity. "We've got a lot of ground to cover. Let's gather as many texts, scrolls, and pages as possible."

With renewed purpose, the group set to work. They carefully pulled ancient tomes and dusty scrolls from the shelves, creating a makeshift workspace amidst the aisles. The air was heavy with the scent of aged paper and the weight of centuries of knowledge.

Ben delicately handled a weathered book, its pages filled with intricate symbols and faded illustrations. "These texts are a treasure trove of information about dark magic. Let's divide and conquer – each of us can take a few and start researching."

Ava nodded in agreement; her hands already occupied with a stack of scrolls. "Agreed. The more we cover, the better our chances of finding a solution."

Holly carefully opened a leather-bound book, her eyes scanning the first pages. "Let's focus on the origins of dark magic. Understanding its roots might give us insight into how to counteract its effects."

Tico chuckled as he browsed through a set of dusty pages, his excitement palpable. "Did you know various civilizations have practiced that dark magic throughout history? It's as if the allure of its power has always been present."

As the group immersed themselves in their research, time seemed to stand still. They delved into the ancient texts, deciphering cryptic incantations, and unraveling the mysteries that lie before them. Their curiosity fueled their efforts, and their understanding grew with each passage they read.

Ben's voice was tinged with amazement as he shared a discovery with the group. "Did you know negative emotions often fuel dark magic? It's as if the darkness within one's heart becomes a source of power."

Ava's fingers danced over an intricate diagram, her eyes widening. "And look at this – it seems that dark magic has a way of spreading like a plague, affecting not only individuals but also the places they inhabit."

Holly's voice was solemn as she read about the consequences of succumbing to dark magic. "The more one delves into the forbidden arts, the harder it becomes to resist its influence. It's a vicious cycle that entraps its victims."

Tico's brow furrowed as he uncovered a particularly grim passage. "There are accounts of dark magic consuming entire civilizations, leading to their downfall. This is a powerful force we're dealing with."

As they continued to research, their sense of urgency grew. The information they uncovered was enlightening and unsettling, shedding light on the true nature of the dark magic that had ensnared Snowflake and the affected dwarves.

Ben's gaze lifted from the pages, his expression resolute. "We're making progress, but we need to find a way to reverse the effects of the dark magic."

Ava nodded, determination burning in her eyes. "We can't let this knowledge go to waste. Let's gather everything we've learned and devise a plan to break the curse."

Holly gently closed a book, her fingers lingering on the aged cover. "We're in a race against time, but we have something invaluable now – knowledge. With it, we have a chance to save Snowflake, the dwarves, and anyone else who may have been affected."

Ben's voice was filled with conviction as he stacked a pile of scrolls. "Let's focus on finding a way to counteract the darkness and free our friends from its grip. We owe it to them."

In a forgotten corner, Tico's keen eyes caught a glimpse of something hidden beneath a dusty bookshelf. He carefully crouched down, his fingers brushing away layers of cobwebs and dust. With a gentle pull, he managed to free a leather-bound book that seemed to have been untouched by human hands for a long time.

The book's cover was weathered, and its pages yellowed with age, giving it an air of mystery and antiquity. Tico's curiosity got the best of him as he opened the book, his eyes scanning the faded words on the pages. His expression quickly shifted from curiosity to astonishment.

His voice, a mixture of disbelief and excitement, called out to his friends, "Hey, you've got to see this!"

Ben, Ava, and Holly gathered around Tico; their eyes fixed on the book's contents. As they read the words, their initial surprise turned into a growing sense of realization and hope. One by one, their faces lit up with a spark of inspiration, as if they had uncovered a hidden treasure.

Tico's finger traced the faded ink on the page as he spoke, his voice tinged with amazement, "This... this could be the solution we've been searching for."

Ava's eyes widened as she read the words aloud, her tone a mixture of wonder and hope, "It says that there's a ritual, a rare and ancient one, that has the power to dispel dark magic and break its hold."

Holly's gaze remained fixed on the pages, a smile tugging at the corners of her lips. "It's a complex process, but if we follow these instructions carefully, we might be able to save Snowflake and the affected dwarves."

Ben's voice held a note of determination as he nodded in agreement. "This is our chance to make things right, to bring an end to the darkness that has gripped our friends."

CHAPTER NINE

Amidst the hallowed shelves, the assembly gathered a diverse group united by a common purpose. Ben stood at the forefront, his eyes reflecting the weight of responsibility. Ava, her aura tinged with magical prowess; Holly, with a penchant for unraveling the threads of the past; and Tico each brought their unique strengths to the table.

Ben, his expression resolute, stepped forward. "Let's not waste time. We have a rare opportunity to free Snowflake and the dwarves from the grip of dark magic. Ava, what insights can you provide about the ritual within the pages of that book?"

Ava, resolute and knowledgeable, boasts a deep understanding of magic and alchemy, inherited from a lineage immersed in the arcane. Her childhood, surrounded by ancient tomes and bubbling potions, laid the foundation for her formidable skills. Renowned for her expertise, Ava's sharp mind and proficiency in the mystical arts make her an invaluable companion, fostering trust among fellow adventurers who rely on her unparalleled knowledge.

Ava, her eyes sparkling, began unraveling the ancient book's mysteries. "The ritual is ancient, its origins obscured by the mists of time. It involves converging elemental forces – earth, air, Fire, and water. Each element represents a facet of magic and must be invoked with precision."

She traced the intricate symbols in the book with her finger, her voice taking on a cadence of arcane wisdom. "The heart of the ritual lies in the balance. If any element is invoked with imbalance, it could amplify the dark magic instead of dispelling it. It's a delicate dance with the forces of nature."

Ben nodded, absorbing the magical intricacies. "Balance is key. We'll need individuals attuned to each element. Holly, any historical context you can provide on the ritual? Anything that might aid our understanding?"

Despite being the youngest, Holly, a magical historian, honed her expertise amid ancient tomes and aromatic herb gardens. Nurtured in a home where history and herbal healing converged, she emerged as a sought-after scholar. Holly's distinctive fusion of botanical and archival knowledge created an enchanting tapestry that seamlessly linked the past, present, and future.

Holly, her fingers gently brushing the frayed edges of an ancient scroll, delved into the historical depths. Raised in a family of herbalists and scholars, Holly's childhood was filled with tales of ancient rituals and forgotten lore. "The ritual has been performed in times of great peril, a beacon of hope when all else seemed lost. But it comes with a cost. The individuals attuned to the elements become vessels of immense magical energy, and the strain on them is tremendous." She recalled her grandmother's stories, whispered by the fireside, about the sacrifices made by those who wielded such power.

She met the gaze of her companions, her eyes carrying the weight of historical awareness. "Legends speak of sacrifices made by those who undertook this quest. To break the shackles of dark magic, one must be prepared to bear a burden beyond the ordinary."

Tico, pragmatic and focused on the immediate challenges, voiced his concern. "Sacrifices we can't avoid, but we must minimize the risks. We can't afford to lose anyone. What about the journey to gather the elemental artifacts? It won't be a walk in the park."

Ava's eyes gleamed with foresight. "The artifacts are scattered across the enchanted forest, guarded by magical creatures and protected by ancient wards. We must navigate carefully, overcoming trials associated with each elemental force."

Ben, now guiding the discussion with the precision of a seasoned leader, addressed the concern. "Tico, we'll need your tactical expertise to plan our route and anticipate the challenges. Holly, gather any information you can find on the locations of these artifacts. Ava, guide us on the magical aspects of the journey."

As the council of minds converged, a tapestry of ideas unfolded. Newly crafted maps became the canvas for intricate plans, with each member offering insights driven by a necessary and unwavering commitment.

The library, silent witness to countless conversations of scholars and seekers, now hosted a different kind of discourse that would shape the destiny of not just the individuals in that room but also the fate of those trapped by dark magic.

In the midst of strategizing, Tico's mind swirled with tactical considerations. The forest was not merely a backdrop for their quest; it was a living entity responding to the ebb and flow of magic. "We need to move with precision. Each step should be calculated, and we must be prepared for the unexpected. The enchanted forest is not known for its hospitality."

Ava, her eyes reflecting the ethereal glow of magical insights, nodded. "Tico is right. The forest is attuned to magic, and it will test us, like it has in the past. Our resolve must be unwavering. Each trial we face will be a reflection of our commitment to the cause."

As the discussions unfolded, Ben found himself reflecting on the influence of leadership. His decisions carried the hopes of those who depended on him, and the burden pressed on his shoulders. "We're not just breaking a curse; we're rewriting destiny. Our choices will echo through time."

Holly, with a historian's perspective, added, "This quest will be inscribed in the annals of the enchanted forest. We are becoming part of its story, just as it becomes part of ours."

Their voices wove a narrative of determination and unity in the labyrinth of bookshelves. Each member of the council brought their strengths to the fore, shaping a plan that was both meticulous and daring. They were not merely adventurers; they were architects of fate, designing a path through the shadows to rescue those held captive by dark magic.

With a plan in place, the adventurers left the hallowed halls of the library, stepping into the enchanted forest that awaited them. The air buzzed with anticipation, and the weight of the ancient ritual hung in the atmosphere like a promise and a challenge.

The journey ahead was perilous, but they walked with purpose, each step echoing with the resolve to reclaim the light that had been eclipsed by darkness. With its secrets and trials, the enchanted forest awaited the arrival of those who dared to defy fate. And in the heart of the ancient library, the books whispered, carrying tales of heroes who rewrote destinies and broke the shackles that bound the realms of magic and reality.

Upon their return, they shared their revelations and captivated the unaffected dwarves with vivid tales of the library and their intricate plan, the adventurers meticulously detailed their strategy to find these hidden artifacts. The dwarves, recognizing the importance of their role, solemnly vowed to watch over Snowflake and the affected dwarves during the adventurers' absence.

Before venturing back into the depths of the forest, Ben, Ava, Tico, and Holly bid heartfelt farewells to their dwarf companions. The adventurers, their minds set on the quest ahead, stepped into the verdant embrace of the woods, leaving behind the dwarven settlement with a shared sense of purpose.

The air was charged with anticipation, and the lush foliage of the enchanted forest rustled as if whispering secrets of their impending journey. Ben, Ava, Holly, and Tico formed a tight-knit group, each bearing the weight of their roles in this perilous quest.

The enchanted forest greeted them with a symphony of colors and magical energies. Giant trees, their trunks twisted with age, towered above like ancient guardians. The air shimmered with iridescent particles, a testament to the magic that infused every leaf and branch.

Ben surveyed the surroundings, his eyes scanning the horizon. "Our first destination is the Grove of Elements. It's said to be the nexus where the elemental forces converge. Ava, any insights on navigating there safely?"

Ava, attuned to the magical currents, closed her eyes, feeling the subtle vibrations in the air. "The Grove is responsive to magical intent. We must approach with respect and balance. Any disruption might alert the magical guardians that protect the elemental artifacts."

As they ventured deeper into the forest, the landscape transformed. They traversed meandering streams, their waters imbued with the essence of the water element. The air grew warmer as they approached a clearing where flames danced without consuming anything—a manifestation of the fire element's presence.

Holly examined the surroundings with a keen eye. "The ancients believed the Grove was a place of equilibrium, where the elements existed in harmony. It's a reflection of the delicate balance we must maintain in our quest."

Tico kept his senses alert for any signs of danger. "Balance is good, but we can't ignore the inherent risks. We're entering the territory of mystical creatures, and they might not take kindly to our intrusion."

The adventurers moved cautiously, guided by the flickering lights that led them to the Grove of Elements. As they entered the clearing, a magical resonance filled the air, and the elements seemed to come alive. Water droplets danced in midair, flames swirled in hypnotic patterns, and the earth beneath their feet pulsed with vitality.

In the heart of the Grove, the elemental artifacts awaited, each guarded by a magical entity. With a determined gleam in his eye, Ben addressed the group, "Our task is clear. Ava, guide us through the magical defenses. Holly, help decipher any clues about the artifacts. Tico, keep a watchful eye for any signs of danger."

Tico, the group's vigilant protector and skilled fighter, hails from an elf-like family deeply connected to the earth. Raised with a balance of strength and intelligence, his agile and brave nature makes him an unwavering guardian. Intrigued by magic and enchanted artifacts from a young age, Tico's dual prowess in combat and mysticism establishes him as a valuable asset, ensuring the safety of the group with his watchful dedication.

As Ava channeled her magical abilities to attune with the protective spells, Holly delved into the ancient scrolls she had brought with her, searching for clues on how to approach the artifacts. Tico, eyes scanning the surroundings, remained vigilant.

The first artifact, a crystal vial containing pure water imbued with the essence of the water element, lay protected by a guardian of liquid light. Ava's hands moved with practiced precision, weaving a tapestry of magic that resonated with the guardian. As the guardian's luminous form softened, they carefully retrieved the crystal vial containing pure water imbued with the essence of the water element.

The water artifact, held within a crystal vial, radiated a serene glow, capturing the essence of flowing rivers and tranquil lakes. Within its depths swirled shimmering currents, reflecting the purity and fluidity of the water element.

Holly deciphered an ancient inscription on the vial. "The undines, water spirits of ancient lore, have blessed this water. It is the essence of purity and healing."

Tico, scanning the perimeter, noticed a shadowy figure lurking in the underbrush. "We're not alone. Dark forces are watching. We need to move quickly."

With the water artifact secured, their path led them to a rugged mountainside where the earth element's artifact lay nestled among ancient stones. As the ground beneath their feet shifted and rumbled, Ava's attunement to the earth's energy guided them through the protective wards. With each step, they felt the steady pulse of the earth's power, until they finally reached the ancient stone pulsating with the essence of the earth element. As they came closer a series of intricate symbols emerged on the surface of the largest stone, forming a mysterious puzzle.

Ben, a hand on the stone, felt a connection to the very heartbeat of the earth. "This stone holds the essence of stability and resilience. It's a foundation upon which the magic of the counter-spell can rest."

With each pulse, Ben deciphered the rhythm of the symbols, recognizing them as the earth's own language. Channeling his connection to the land, Ben manipulated the stones, aligning them in harmony with the earth's heartbeat. As the final piece fell into place, the stone's surface shimmered with golden light, revealing the ancient artifact pulsating with the essence of the earth element. With a reverent touch, Ben claimed the artifact, its power echoing with the steady beat of the earth beneath his feet.

The earth artifact, a weathered stone of immense proportions, exuded an aura of timeless strength and stability. Carved with intricate symbols, it seemed to emanate the very essence of the earth itself. Its surface, rough yet resilient, bore the marks of eons of existence, a testament to the enduring power of the earth element.

Their journey led them to a cavern bathed in flickering flames, where the fire artifact awaited amidst dancing tendrils of heat. As the air grew warmer and the flames beckoned them closer, a sense of unease settled over Holly, her fear of fire palpable in the stifling heat. The element seemed to sense her trepidation, fueling the flames with an intensity that made the task ahead seem insurmountable.

Observing the flames with timid yet scholarly curiosity, Holly murmured, "Fire is both destructive and transformative. This artifact embodies the essence of change."

Undeterred by the daunting challenge, Ava and Tico pooled their magical abilities, creating a shield of swirling winds to protect them from the intense heat. With Ava's expertise in elemental magic and Tico's mastery over illusions, they worked in tandem to navigate the fiery labyrinth surrounding the artifact.

However, as they neared the heart of the inferno, a sudden surge of flame caught Tico off guard, searing his hand with a painful burn. Gritting his teeth against the pain, Tico pushed forward, his determination unwavering despite the agony.

With synchronized movements and unwavering resolve, Ava and Tico reached out and grasped the fire artifact, their combined magic quelling the flames and securing their prize. Though the journey had tested their limits, they emerged victorious, the fire artifact safely in their possession.

The fire artifact manifested as a shimmering ember, glowing with the intensity of a roaring inferno. Within its fiery core, swirling hues of crimson and gold danced in an eternal dance, embodying the dual nature of destruction and renewal. As they gazed upon its mesmerizing flames, they felt the raw power of the fire element, a force both fearsome and awe-inspiring in its fiery embrace.

Tico, nursing a scorched hand, still ever cautious, noticed the shadows closing in. "We're being observed. Dark entities are testing our resolve. Keep your guard up."

Their quest led them deeper into the heart of the forest, where the air hummed with the unseen currents of the air element. As they approached the final artifact, an ethereal feather glowing with the essence of the wind, they found themselves surrounded by swirling eddies of air that seemed to shield the artifact from their grasp.

Holly, her connection to the water element strong, created a barrier of liquid light that warded off the turbulent winds. Ben, his bond with the earth element unwavering, anchored them to the ground, providing stability amidst the chaos. Tico, still nursing his scorched hand from the fire artifact's trial, summoned a protective barrier of flames to shield them from the fiercest gusts.

Ava, in tune with the magic that flowed through the artifacts, guided them through the intricate patterns that protected the feather. Yet, despite their combined efforts, the air element's presence remained formidable, resisting their every attempt to claim the artifact.

As they stood on the brink of defeat, Ben, his resolve strengthened by the bonds he shared with his companions, stepped forward. With a steadfast commitment born from his connection to the earth, he braved the tempestuous winds, each movement a testament to his unwavering dedication.

With Ava's guidance and the support of his friends, Ben reached out and claimed the feather, its delicate form pulsating with the boundless power of the wind.

As Ben held the feather, he felt a gentle breeze caress his face. "Air, the breath of life. This feather embodies the freedom that comes with breaking the shackles of dark magic."

With a knowing smile, Holly added, "Legends say that a mythical creature, a guardian of the skies, once carried this feather. It symbolizes the release from the chains that bind."

The air artifact materialized as an ethereal feather, its delicate form radiating with a soft, iridescent glow that mirrored the ever-changing hues of the sky. Light as a whisper, yet imbued with the boundless power of the wind, it seemed to dance on unseen currents, embodying the freedom and unpredictability of the air element.

As Ben handed the feather to Ava, a sense of triumph washed over them, they felt a sense of awe and reverence for the elemental forces that had guided them on their journey.

Tico, his gaze now fixed on the shifting shadows, issued a warning. "Our presence here has attracted more than just the guardians of the artifacts. We need to leave before we're overwhelmed."

The adventurers retreated from the Grove of Elements, each carrying an elemental artifact that pulsated with magical energy. The forest, alive with whispers and unseen eyes, seemed to close in on them. Ben, his leadership unmatched, addressed the group, "Our next destination is the Ruins of Arcane Insight. Holly, any insights on what challenges might await us there?"

Holly, her eyes distant as if peering into the annals of time, spoke, "The ruins are a repository of ancient knowledge, guarded by arcane constructs and spectral guardians. We must tread carefully and respect the wisdom that lingers within."

The journey to the ruins led them through twisting paths and hidden clearings, the air thick with a sense of foreboding. As they entered the ancient ruins, a hush fell over the group. The crumbling stone structures bore witness to the passage of countless ages, and the remnants of forgotten spells lingered in the air.

Ava, her magical senses tingling, warned of the arcane defenses ahead. "The ruins are attuned to the ebb and flow of magic. Any misstep might trigger ancient wards. Ben, your leadership will be crucial here."

Ben, the adept leader of the group, grew up in a village of arcane mysteries, where his sharp intellect and innate magical affinity made him a natural leader. Renowned for his wit and an exceptional ability to solve puzzles and perceive hidden connections, Ben's high IQ and mastery of magic set him apart. A voracious reader of ancient texts, he effortlessly guided his companions through the most perplexing challenges, establishing himself as an indispensable leader among adventurers.

Ben, a determined glint in his eyes, led the group through the ruins, avoiding the spectral guardians that stirred with every step. Holly, her fingers tracing ancient glyphs, deciphered the cryptic messages that adorned the walls.

Tico kept an eye on the shadows. "These ruins are a treasure trove of forgotten spells. We might find clues here that could aid us in our quest."

As they delved deeper, they uncovered a hidden chamber adorned with symbols of starlight. In the center lay the Starlight Orb, a crystalline sphere that radiated the essence of the cosmos. Ava, her hands glowing with magical energy, navigated the protective spells that guarded the artifact.

Holly, studying the symbols etched into the walls, whispered, "The Starlight Orb is said to hold the knowledge of the stars. It's a beacon that illuminates the path through the darkest realms of magic."

With the Starlight Orb secured, the adventurers faced their next challenge—the Hidden Vale of Beasts. Tico, ever watchful, voiced his concern. "This place is teeming with magical creatures. We can't afford to underestimate them."

The air crackled with unseen energies as they ventured into the Hidden Vale. The flora and fauna seemed to pulse with a mystical heartbeat, and the eyes of hidden creatures gleamed in the shadows. Ben's sharp senses guided the group through the labyrinth of magical beings.

Ava, her magical aura a shield against hostile energies, murmured, "These creatures are guardians of the vale, each with a role in maintaining the delicate balance of magic. We must tread lightly."

Holly, with a historian's insight, recognized the significance of the creatures they encountered. "Legends speak of the Vale Keepers, beings bound to the magic of this realm. They test the hearts of those who enter, ensuring that only those who are worthy pass through."

Tico, his hand on the hilt of his blade, remained alert. "Worthiness doesn't guarantee safety. These creatures might see us as intruders. Stay on guard."

The adventurers faced trials of character as they traversed the Hidden Vale. The Vale Keepers, manifestations of the mystical beings that dwelled in this hidden realm, tested their resolve. With a firm but fair hand, Ben navigated diplomatic encounters with creatures whose motives were as enigmatic as the magic surrounding them.

Ava, with a touch that soothed both magical and mundane anxieties, communicated with the spirits of the vale. Holly, with a scholar's patience, sought to understand the cultural tapestry woven by these mystical beings.

Tico, pragmatic and vigilant, ensured that their journey through the vale did not attract the attention of darker forces that might exploit the chaos of magical encounters.

In the heart of the vale, they reached the final destination—the Moonlit Altar. The altar, bathed in the soft glow of moonlight, held the key to unlocking the ancient ritual. With his gaze fixed on the altar, and Ben felt the weight of destiny pressing on him. "This is where it all comes together. Ava, the artifacts. Holly, the historical context. Tico, keep watch. We can't afford any surprises."

As Ava arranged the elemental artifacts around the Moonlit Altar, the air hummed with magic. Holly, her fingers tracing the symbols on the altar, began to decipher the ritual inscriptions. Tico, eyes scanning the surroundings, remained vigilant.

The moon, a celestial witness, cast its silvery glow on the altar as Ava activated the ritual with a surge of magical energy. The artifacts resonated harmoniously, and the altar shimmered with an otherworldly light.

Her eyes reflecting the depth of historical awareness, Holly whispered, "This is a ritual of renewal, a dance with the forces that shape reality. We are rewriting the story of the enchanted forest."

Tico, his hand kept on the hilt of his blade, kept a watchful eye on the surroundings. "Let's not celebrate yet. The ritual might attract attention."

As the ritual unfolded, a dark presence stirred in the shadows. The air crackled with malevolence, and the enchanted forest seemed to hold its breath. Ben, his gaze unwavering, faced the looming darkness. "We knew this wouldn't be easy. Stand ready."

The culmination of their journey had brought them to the threshold of a confrontation with the very forces that sought to shroud the enchanted forest in darkness. The Moonlit Altar, bathed in celestial radiance, stood as a beacon of hope in the heart of a realm teetering on the edge of magic

and despair. The adventurers, bound by a shared purpose and tested by the trials of their quest, prepared to face the impending darkness, and reclaim the light that had been lost.

As the moon's glow intensified, shadows seemed to writhe with an ominous presence. The enchanted forest, holding its breath, appeared aware of an impending threat. Tico's vigilant eyes darted between the shadows, while Holly's historical insights whispered of ancient conflicts etched into the realm.

Suddenly, a dark force emerged, tendrils of malice coiling around the Moonlit Altar. Ben's gaze met the looming darkness, and he braced the group. "Prepare yourselves. The ritual has drawn more than just our allies."

Just as the adventurers readied for an imminent battle, the dark magic, sensing their readiness, abruptly retreated. The air, thick with tension, settled into an eerie stillness. Bewilderment replaced determination on the faces of Ben, Ava, Holly, and Tico. The enchanted forest, seemingly untouched by the recent threat, sighed in relief.

Unbeknownst to the adventurers, the dark magic had merely slithered away, biding its time in the shadows. The confrontation they braced for had been averted, yet the malevolence that sought to consume the enchanted forest now lingered elsewhere, patient, and insidious. As the adventurers exchanged uncertain glances, a distant echo hinted at the dark magic's lingering presence, leaving the group on edge, poised for the unknown challenges that lay ahead.

Chapter Ten

As Ben, Ava, Holly, and Tico made their way back to Snowflake and the other dwarves, they hoped that the ritual served its purpose. Ben's mind raced with a whirlwind of thoughts, his earlier confidence now tinged with doubt. Had they truly succeeded in lifting the dark magic's curse? The weight of responsibility pressed heavily on his shoulders, a constant reminder of the stakes.

A shadow fell over a quaint village nearby as rumors of the dark magic curse spread like wildfire. Whispers echoed through the cobbled streets, and terror clung to the air like a shroud. The once- close-knit community was now fractured by uncertainty, and the faces of the villagers bore expressions of dread and suspicion.

Snowflake's home, nestled in the forest, became a focal point of apprehension. The villagers, driven by superstition, viewed the dwelling as the epicenter of the malevolent force that had befallen their community.

As the sun dipped below the horizon, casting long shadows over the village, a procession of worried villagers approached Snowflake's home. Torches flickered in the gathering gloom, their flames mirroring the growing tension in the air. The adventurers, returning from their quest with artifacts pulsating with magical energy, sensed the unrest that gripped the village.

Ben whispered to his companions, "We're just in time. The villagers seem to have decided that Snowflake's home is the source of the curse." He couldn't shake the gnawing worry that they might have been too late to prevent further harm.

Ava replied, "Panic has blinded them. We need to defuse the situation before it spirals out of control." Her heart ached for the villagers, who were as much victims of the curse as those directly affected by it.

Holly observed, "Dread is a potent force. It can drive communities to acts of desperation. We must tread carefully." She remembered the tales of other villages torn apart by fear and hoped they could avoid a similar fate.

Tico added, "We can't let them harm Snowflake and the dwarves. Let's approach cautiously and try to reason with them." His protective instincts flared, fueled by his commitment to their mission.

As the adventurers approached the scene, the murmurs among the villagers grew louder. Accusatory glances were cast toward Snowflake's home, where the affected dwarves, unaware of the impending danger, went about their daily routines.

The village elder, a figure of authority among the crowd, stepped forward, his voice carrying a tremor of apprehension. "The curse has taken hold of those living in this cottage. They are responsible for capturing and torturing some of our fellow townsfolk! We can't let it spread further. The source must be eradicated!"

A ripple of agreement passed through the villagers, their fear fueling a collective resolve to rid themselves of the perceived threat. The adventurers, pushing through the crowd, faced a sea of anxious faces.

Steady in his voice, Ben addressed the crowd, "We understand your concerns, but there is no need to act drastically. We've gathered information about the curse and are working on a solution." He fought to keep his voice calm, despite the anxiety gnawing at him.

A villager's face contorted with anger, retorted, "Words won't undo the curse. We've seen strange things happen around here over the past couple of days, and every single occurrence has Snowflake and those dwarves' prints all over it. It's a blight on our land."

Ava implored, "Magic is a complex force. Hasty actions can make things worse. Give us time to find a solution that doesn't harm innocents. We have made a lot of progress already, and if we just wait a little longer, the curse should lift away in due time." She hoped her words could reach the hearts of those driven by fear.

Tico, scanning the crowd, sensed the volatility. "We need to act fast. If they decide to take matters into their own hands, we won't be able to stop them."

As the adventurers tried to reason with the villagers, a murmur spread through the crowd—a dissenting voice rising above the collective fear. It was a villager, an older woman with wrinkled hands that spoke of years of toil. Her gaze held a mix of compassion and defiance.

"I understand your grievances, but they're part of our village. We can't turn against them. Let's not bring darkness into our hearts with our own hands," she pleaded, her words resonating with a few hearts in the crowd.

The village elder hesitated. The crowd, a volatile mix of emotions, wavered on the edge of a precipice.

In that moment of uncertainty, a lone figure emerged from the shadows. It was Snowflake, her eyes wide with innocence, unaware of the turmoil surrounding her. The affected dwarves, following her lead, stood with a curious innocence that clashed with the charged atmosphere.

His voice cutting through the tense air, Ben shouted, "Stop! You're about to commit a grave mistake. Let us handle this."

But the unrest that gripped the villagers had reached a boiling point. Torches were raised, and a villager, consumed by hysteria, hurled a burning brand toward Snowflake's home. The flames caught on the thatched roof, licking hungrily at the structure.

Chaos erupted. The adventurers rushed forward, desperate to quell the spreading fire and protect Snowflake and the dwarves.

Tico, his voice a fierce command, shouted at the villagers, "What are you doing? You're destroying the homes of your own people!"

The village elder, remorse written on his face, tried to restore order. The flames roared, casting a flickering glow on the anguished faces of the villagers.

The adventurers, their efforts to douse the flames hampered by the crowd, felt the weight of impending tragedy. Snowflake reached out toward the burning home, a cry of innocence lost in the uproar.

Once the flames descended into mere clouds of smoke, the village fell into stunned silence, the echoes of uneasiness slowly dissipating. The once-fiery crowd now faced the consequences of their actions, and the reality of the damage inflicted on their community began to sink in.

Snowflake stood beside the charred remains of her home. The affected dwarves, huddled together in confusion, looked toward the adventurers for guidance.

Ben addressed the villagers, "Apprehension led you to the brink of disaster. Your magical or mundane differences shouldn't tear your community apart."

The village elder, a sad figure in the aftermath, nodded reluctantly. The villagers, their initial anger replaced by remorse, began to disperse, each carrying the burden of their actions.

As the adventurers surveyed the scene, they knew their quest was far from over. The village, scarred by the flames of fear, needed healing. The darkness momentarily consumed their hearts and had to be replaced with the light of compassion. The journey to dispel the curse extended beyond the realm of magic and into the very fabric of the human spirit.

Ben's thoughts drifted back to the beginning of their quest, the initial hope that had driven them. He resolved that they would not let fear and darkness prevail. This was a fight for the soul of the village, for the bonds that connected them all.

Snowflake, her eyes reflecting the devastation and hope intertwined, whispered, "We can rebuild. We have to."

Ben, Ava, Holly, and Tico stood near the remains, their faces a tableau of mixed emotions. The destruction was undeniable, but a surprising hush had fallen over the enchanted forest. An eerie calm replaced the expected wails of anguish and despair.

Snowflake emerged from the shadows, confused and in a slight daze. Behind her, the affected dwarves shook their heads as if waking up from a dream.

"What… happened?" Snowflake blinked, trying to make sense of the situation. "I felt like I was being kept prisoner by my thoughts…"

Ava murmured, "Wait… The curse… it's gone. The magical residue that clung to the house and nearby trees, it's dissipated."

Holly surveyed the smoldering ruins, her mind racing to comprehend the unexpected turn of events. "But how? Burning the hut wasn't supposed to break the curse. Could it have been the ritual's doing?"

Tico scanned the surroundings. "This doesn't make sense. Dark magic doesn't just vanish. It fights back, resisting any attempts to dispel it."

Ben, his gaze fixed on the little that remained of Snowflake's hut, voiced the uncertainty that hung in the air. "We achieved our goal, but at what cost?"

A few remaining villagers, their expressions a mix of relief and confusion, approached cautiously.

As the adventurers and villagers gathered, a subtle shift occurred in the enchanted forest. The air now carried a whisper of renewal. The trees, their leaves rustling with an almost soothing melody, responded to the unspoken questions that lingered in the hearts of those who had witnessed the burning.

Snowflake, her voice a delicate thread in the quietude, spoke, "The forest... it mourns, but it also heals. We might have lost our physical shelter, but perhaps we gained something else."

Ava added, "Dark Magic is unpredictable. It adapts and evolves. Maybe the destruction of the hut disrupted its hold, sent it scattering into the ether."

Holly, her gaze distant as she contemplated the unexpected twist, whispered, "The forest, it's ancient and wise. Maybe it recognized the sacrifice and chose to cleanse itself. Magic is as much about intent as it is about rituals."

Tico, pragmatic as ever, couldn't help but voice a lingering doubt, "But what about the villagers? They won't understand this. To them, it might seem like their actions were justified."

Ben, wrestling with the situation's complexities, stepped forward. "We need to address the villagers. We can't let misunderstanding breed further discord. We might have an opportunity to bridge the gap that divides us."

As the adventurers moved to address the assembled crowd, the enchanted forest seemed to cradle the remnants of the burned hut. The villagers, expressions of a mosaic of emotions, awaited an explanation for the unforeseen events.

Facing the expectant gazes, Ben spoke with a measured tone, "The curse is broken. The forest has responded, and the darkness has lifted."

The village leader, his features a mask of disbelief, stepped forward. "This... it wasn't what we expected. We came to cleanse the land, not witness some mysterious magic at play."

Ava, attempting to bridge the gap, explained, "Magic is not always straightforward. It's as much a force of nature as the enchanted forest itself. Sometimes, actions that seem destructive lead to unexpected outcomes."

Holly also addressed the crowd, "What we need now is unity. We've all witnessed something extraordinary. Instead of letting misgivings divide us, let it be the catalyst for our unity."

A fragile peace settled over the enchanted forest in the aftermath of the burning. As the first rays of dawn touched the smoldering ruins, a symbol of both loss and renewal, the enchanted forest seemed to embrace the community. The scars of the past lingered, but the potential for a harmonious future beckoned, a testament to the resilience of a village bound by both magic and the shared trials that tested the very fabric of their existence.

The morning sun cast a warm glow over the rubble of Snowflake's hut, now reduced to large sections of charred timbers and ashes. The enchanted forest, though scarred, held a quiet inner strength as if whispering secrets only the ancient trees could comprehend.

Holly knelt beside the burnt embers, her fingers tracing the ashen remains. "This wasn't a typical magical combustion. There's something intricate about how the magic interacted with the flames."

Ava nodded in agreement. "It's almost as if the forest intervened, balancing destruction with restoration. But that's not how curses work; they don't typically resolve themselves."

Tico surveyed the scene with a critical eye. "We need to figure out what really happened before rumors and misunderstandings spread again."

Ben contemplated the unfolding mystery. "We need more information. We'll talk to witnesses, examine the remains, and consult the ancient texts in the library. There has to be an explanation for what transpired."

As the group fanned out to investigate, their minds buzzed with questions. Snowflake and a few villagers who had witnessed the chaotic events offered their accounts. The villagers, still wary but now open to helping, shared their perspectives.

The adventurers reconvened in the heart of the village, their faces reflecting the situation's complexity. Ava, her expression a mix of fascination and confusion, shared her findings. "The magical residue here was unlike anything I've encountered. It was as if the very fabric of the curse unraveled and dispersed into the forest."

Holly interjected, "I've heard of this before. There's mention of a rare phenomenon, an inherent balance in certain magical realms. When dark magic reaches a point of extreme imbalance, the environment might attempt to correct it."

Tico, leaning against a charred beam, contemplated the implications. "So, the forest fought back against the curse. That explains the unexpected resolution, but it doesn't tell us why or how or if the ritual solved it all."

Ben, absorbing the information, guided the group's focus. "We can't rely on the forest to solve our problems. We need to understand the curse itself and its vulnerabilities. Only then can we ensure a lasting solution."

The adventurers' collective wisdom expanded as they delved into the tomes and scrolls gathered from the ancient library. The pages of these arcane volumes and the very air they breathed became permeated with the fragrance of time-aged parchment, as if the knowledge contained within eagerly anticipated their relentless pursuit of understanding. In the midst of a mystical circle formed by Ava, Holly, and Tico, Ben vocalized the imperative nature of their quest, the urgency hanging palpably in the charged atmosphere.

"The forest might have given us a reprieve, but we can't rely on chance. We need to confront the dark magic head-on. What does the magical residue tell you about the curse's nature?"

Ava, her fingers gently tracing the notes she had taken, began deciphering the magical signatures. "The curse is intricate, interwoven into the very essence of the enchanted forest. It draws power from negative emotions, but it's not an independent entity. It's more like a malignant force that permeates the very heart of the land."

Holly added a layer of context. "If the curse is tied to the land, disrupting its balance could trigger unforeseen consequences. The forest intervened, but it might not be a reliable ally. We need to find the root of the curse and neutralize it."

Tico proposed a tactical approach. "We know the curse draws power from negative emotions. Let's exploit that. We can create a diversion, draw its attention, and strike where it's most vulnerable."

Ben, synthesizing their insights, outlined the plan. "We'll gather the villagers, prepare defenses, and create a concentrated source of negative emotions. Meanwhile, Ava will work on a counter- spell to weaken the curse's grip. We need to be ready for whatever the curse throws at us."

As the plan unfolded, the adventurers faced the challenging task of persuading the wary villagers, who harbored reservations about magic. With eloquent presentations and heartfelt assurances, the adventurers successfully convinced the villagers to join their cause. Together, in a newfound unity, they worked in tandem, raising defenses and invoking ancient incantations to confront the impending challenge that loomed before them.

As night descended upon the enchanted forest, the air pulsated with an electric anticipation. The adventurers, villagers, and Snowflake with her dwarves convened, prepared to plunge into the heart of the mystical woodland. A solemn ambiance enveloped them, the collective weight of their shared trials etched visibly on the faces of those who had braved the tempest together.

The enchanted forest seemed to pulse with silent energy as if acknowledging the courage of those who stood against the encroaching darkness. Ben, his gaze firm, addressed the assembly.

"We face a formidable foe, but we face it together. The curse has touched our lives but won't define our destiny. We fight for our home, our history, and the magic that binds us."

Ava, her hands aglow with magical energy, stepped forward. "We have a plan, but we must stay vigilant. The curse adapts, so we must be ready to adapt to it. Our unity is our strength."

Her voice resonates with ancient wisdom, and Holly added, "In the heart of every curse lies vulnerability. We must find it, expose it, and free the enchanted forest from the grip of darkness."

Tico concluded, "This is our final confrontation. We'll face challenges but emerge victorious. For the enchanted forest, our friends, and the adaptability that binds us."

As the team hardened themselves for the looming confrontation, the enchanted forest held its breath. The final battle against the curse awaited, a test of courage, unity, and the firm belief that even the darkest magic could be dispelled by the light of hope.

Chapter Eleven

The enchanted forest buzzed with tension as the villagers, Snowflake, the dwarves, and the adventurers gathered at the edge of the dense woodland. A sense of strength pulsed through the air, mingling with the crackle of magic and the distant rumble of thunder.

Ben, Ava, Holly, and Tico stood at the forefront, their expressions a mix of resolve and apprehension. They knew that the looming battle against the dark magic would test their strength, their unity, and their belief in the power of light to overcome the shadows.

Ben's mind raced with the weight of leadership. Every decision he made carried the hopes of those who depended on him. The burden pressed heavily on his shoulders, but he refused to let it break him. This was a fight for their friends, for the village, and for the enchanted forest itself.

"We must proceed with caution," Ben cautioned, his voice carrying a weight of responsibility. "The dark magic is formidable, but together, we can overcome it." He drew strength from the unwavering support of his companions, knowing that their bond was their greatest weapon.

Ava nodded, her eyes alight with determination. "We need to lure it out into the open where we can confront it directly. Holly, Tico, can you create distractions to draw its attention?" She felt a deep connection to the magical currents that flowed through the forest, a reminder of the power they wielded for good.

Holly nodded, her staff already crackling with magical energy. "I'll conjure illusions to confuse and disorient it. Tico, you focus on creating noise and chaos to keep it off balance." She remembered the ancient stories of heroes who had faced similar trials, drawing inspiration from their courage.

Tico grinned, cracking his knuckles. "Leave it to me. I'll make enough racket to wake the dead." He relished the opportunity to protect his friends, channeling his fear into a fierce determination.

With their plan in place, the adventurers turned to the villagers, Snowflake, and the dwarves, their faces a mixture of fear and willpower.

"We'll need your help to create a barrier around the dark magic once it's lured out," Ben explained. "Stay close, and follow our lead. Together, we can contain it." He felt a surge of pride in the villagers' willingness to stand with them, a testament to the resilience of their community.

The villagers nodded, their expressions grim but resolute. They had seen firsthand the devastation wrought by the dark magic and were eager to play their part in banishing it from their land.

The air crackled with an arcane energy, and with a shared look, the adventurers and their allies advanced further into the heart of the forest. Their footsteps were muffled by the thick undergrowth, but every rustle of leaves and snap of twigs carried an undertone of warning, echoing through the enchanted surroundings like a mystical prelude to the challenges awaiting them.

As they approached the series of rock formations where the dark magic was rumored to be hiding, a sense of foreboding washed over them. The air grew thick with an oppressive energy, and the sky overhead darkened with ominous clouds.

"We're getting close," Ava whispered, her senses attuned to the subtle shifts in the magical currents. "Be on your guard." She felt a deep responsibility to her friends and the village, a determination to see their mission through.

Suddenly, a bolt of lightning split the sky, illuminating the rock formations ahead with an eerie glow. Thunder rumbled ominously, shaking the ground beneath their feet.

"We've got its attention," Holly said, her voice tinged with excitement. "Now, let's give it something to focus on." She felt a surge of exhilaration, knowing they were on the cusp of a pivotal moment.

With a wave of her staff, she conjured illusions that danced and flickered among the rocks, twisting and morphing into grotesque shapes. Tico followed suit, unleashing a cacophony of noise that reverberated through the forest, setting birds to flight and animals to scatter.

The dark magic, sensing the disturbance, intensified, swirling around them with newfound ferocity. Lightning streaked across the sky, illuminating the twisted forms of trees that loomed like sentinels of the dark magic that permeated the atmosphere.

Shadows twisted and contorted, conjoining into a colossal form that loomed over the battlefield. The ground continued to tremble beneath its malevolent presence, and the air crackled once more with an intensity that sent shivers down the spines of all who stood against it.

Ava's eyes widened with realization. "This is the source! We have to face it together!" She felt a surge of determination, knowing that their unity was their greatest strength.

The colossal figure descended upon them with an overwhelming force, its dark tendrils reaching out to ensnare the team and their allies. The battle that ensued was fierce and chaotic, as the group struggled against the relentless onslaught of dark magic.

Ava, her gaze sharp despite the distorted visibility, sensed a wicked presence closing in. "Be on guard," she warned, her voice carried away by the wind. "Something is watching us."

Just as her words faded into the storm's roar, shadows emerged from the tempest, merging into sinister figures that moved with an otherworldly grace. Cloaked in darkness, these spectral entities advanced, their movements synchronized with the dance of the storm.

Tico unsheathed his dagger, his senses heightened as he assessed the approaching threat. "Dark magic has summoned these creatures," he declared, his voice firm above the howling wind. "Be ready for anything." He felt a fierce protectiveness over his friends, channeling his fear into a resolve to protect.

However, just as despair threatened to take hold, a chorus of battle cries erupted from the depths of the tempest. The unaffected dwarfs charged into the fray alongside the villagers and Snowflake. The dwarfs swung their axes with precision, their strength unmatched as they clashed with the shadowy figures emerging from the storm.

Snowflake conjured radiant shards of magical ice, casting a radiant glow that cut through the darkness. The enchanted ice pierced through the spectral entities, leaving a trail of crystalline frost in its wake. The villagers, armed with makeshift weapons, fought valiantly, their courage bolstered by the unexpected reinforcements.

Yet, as the team joined forces with the dwarfs, the forest itself seemed to rebel. Once benevolent animals now twisted by the dark magic emerged, their eyes gleaming with an unnatural malevolence. Deer, rabbits, and birds, now corrupted by the menacing energy, charged at the combined group with a ferocity that belied their once-docile nature.

Ava, her telepathic connection reaching out to the affected creatures, sensed their internal struggle. "They're not truly evil," she exclaimed, her voice desperate to convey the creatures' plight. "The dark magic has corrupted them. We must find a way to break its hold!" Her heart ached for the creatures, knowing they were victims of the same malevolent force.

Then, in a cruel twist of fate, amidst the chaotic maelstrom of dark magic, Ava, the indomitable force within the group, found herself ensnared by the evil energy. Seemingly overpowered, she faltered, her once-unyielding strength waning against the overwhelming force that sought to engulf her. The air, thick with the oppressive presence of the dark magic, began to escape her lungs, leaving her gasping for breath. Her eyes, filled with desperation, sought out Ben, her steadfast companion, as if signaling that all hope was slipping away.

Ava struggled against the dark magic, her every effort met with resistance, she found herself teetering on the precipice of death. The shadows clung to her, their tendrils wrapping around her like a suffocating shroud.

Yet, just when despair threatened to consume them all, a seismic surge of energy erupted from Ben. His mind flashed with a memory, in the ancient library, he had come across a passage about channeling one's latent magic. With this newfound understanding, he focused on that knowledge, allowing the energy within him to surge forth.

Drawing upon this wellspring of arcane wisdom, he unleashed a torrent of his own magic. The air vibrated with intensity as the pulsating energy manifested into a protective barrier, a shimmering shield that surrounded Ava at the last possible moment.

Ben's eyes blazed with purpose as he defied the encroaching darkness. The protective barrier he conjured not only shielded Ava but radiated a brilliant light that pushed back the oppressive shadows. The clash between his newfound power and the malevolent force created a spectacle that seemed to echo through the very fabric of the enchanted forest.

Ava, held within the sanctuary of the protective barrier, felt the immediate reprieve from the suffocating grip of the dark magic. As the tendrils recoiled, their malevolence thwarted, she took a gasping breath, her eyes locking onto Ben with a mixture of gratitude and awe.

The rest of the group, momentarily paralyzed by the intensity of the unfolding drama, snapped back into action. Snowflake unleashed a cascade of magical ice, the dwarfs swung their axes with renewed vigor, and the villagers rallied behind the resilient adventurers.

As the malevolent energy recoiled from the resilience of the protective barrier, a renewed sense of hope surged through the group. Ava, now regaining her composure within the sheltering light, nodded to Ben with silent gratitude. The bond between them, forged through countless trials, had once again proven unbreakable.

Ben, his staff at the ready, scanned the chaotic battlefield. "Snowflake, use your powers to create a barrier. Protect the villagers and dwarfs. We'll handle the corrupted creatures!" His determination to see this through to the end burned brightly.

Snowflake nodded, her hands swirling with magical energy. A shimmering dome of ice encased the villagers and dwarfs, shielding them from the onslaught of dark magic-infused animals. With newfound purpose, the team focused on freeing the corrupted creatures from the clutches of the dark magic.

Holly, armed with her knowledge of herbs, crafted a concoction that emitted a calming aroma. She tossed the mixture towards the oncoming animals, hoping to break the enchantment. The fragrance permeated the air, causing a momentary hesitation in the creatures' relentless advance.

Seizing the opportunity, Tico and Ben moved with skilled coordination. Tico darted through the chaos, swiftly collecting Moonleaf leaves from the trees once again. Ben utilized his staff to harness his recently discovered latent magic, crafting a protective barrier that enveloped the affected animals. This barrier emitted a resonance with an opposing force, enhancing its defensive properties.

Tico scattered the Moonleaf leaves into the wind, their silvery glow weaving through the air. As the leaves settled on the corrupted creatures, a subtle change occurred. The malevolent gleam in their eyes dimmed, replaced by a flicker of confusion and vulnerability.

Ava, her telepathic link expanding, projected calming thoughts and emotions towards the affected animals. "You are not alone. Fight against the darkness within."

The corrupted creatures, caught in the crossfire between the enchanting Moonleaf and Ava's soothing telepathic influence, began to regain control over their senses. Slowly, the aggression faded, and the once-twisted animals retreated, leaving behind a forest restored to its eerie but natural calm.

Recognizing the waning strength of the dark magic as the adventurers relentlessly pressed forward, Snowflake, with a decisive sweep of her hands, dispelled the barrier of ice that had cocooned the villagers.

Sensing the imminent defeat of the malevolent force, she understood that the time had come for the villagers to lend their aid. The crystalline barrier, once a shield against the encroaching darkness, now dissolved, allowing the liberated villagers to join the final push against the weakened but still formidable remnants of the dark magic.

"Now's our chance!" Ben shouted, his voice cutting through the chaos. "Everyone, follow me!"

With a surge of adrenaline, the adventurers and their allies charged forward, their footsteps pounding against the forest floor. They encircled the dark magic, creating a barrier of bodies and magic to contain it.

"Keep it distracted!" Ava called out, her hands glowing with magical energy as she worked to strengthen the barrier. "We need more time to lure it into the bottle!"

The villagers, Snowflake, and the dwarves heeded her command, redoubling their efforts to create chaos and confusion. The dark magic roared and thrashed against its confines, lashing out with tendrils of shadow and bolts of lightning.

But the adventurers held firm, their purpose unyielding. With each passing moment, they drew the dark magic closer to the waiting bottle, its mouth gaping wide like a hungry maw.

"We're almost there!" Holly shouted, her voice barely received above the roar of the storm. "Just a little closer!"

With a final surge of effort, the adventurers pushed the dark magic toward the waiting bottle, its inky depths swirling with promise.

And then, with a deafening roar, the dark magic was sucked into the bottle, its howls of rage echoing through the forest. The adventurers sealed the bottle tight, their hands trembling with exhaustion and relief.

"We did it," Ben breathed, his voice filled with awe. "We banished the dark magic from the forest."

Ava nodded, her eyes shining with pride. "But our work isn't done yet. We must ensure that it never returns."

Snowflake, surrounded by the dwarves, stood amidst the rock formations, her eyes gleaming with hope.

As the last echoes of the battle subsided, the team and their newfound allies surveyed the aftermath. The dwarfs, villagers, and Snowflake stood amidst the remnants of the enchanted storm, their expressions a mix of exhaustion and triumph. The forest, though scarred by the recent struggle, seemed to breathe a sigh of relief, the magic-infused tempest dissipating into a gentle rain.

Ava, her eyes reflecting the weight of the encounter, addressed the group, "We've faced the dark magic head-on and prevailed. But the forest is still in turmoil. We must press on, find the source of this malevolence, and put an end to it."

As they departed the enchanted forest and ventured back to the hut and clearing nestled where Snowflake and the dwarves called home, a sense of tentative harmony lingered among the adventurers.

However, from this newfound unity Snowflake's gaze darted around the scene, her brow furrowed with growing concern. A sudden realization etched across her face as she scanned the area noticing an exposed gap in the mosaic of their hut, and the absence of a singular dwarf. This dwarf, whose integral presence had intricately woven through the fabric of their shared experiences, now left a noticeable void, a revelation that struck with unexpected force.

Snowflakes' voice, tinged with unease, broke the post-battle silence, "Has anyone seen Swift? I can't find him anywhere."

Ava, scanning the surroundings, exchanged worried glances with the others. "We were so focused on dispersing the darkness that we didn't realize Swift was missing. How did we overlook this?"

Her eyes reflecting a mixture of regret and urgency, Holly added, "In the chaos and confusion, he must have slipped away unnoticed. We need to find him."

Tico voiced the concern that gripped them all. "And what if he took something with him? Something that could be dangerous."

The revelation hung in the air, a shadow cast over the fragile peace that had settled over the enchanted forest. Snowflake, her eyes wide with worry, gathered the other dwarves, their expressions shifting from hope to concern as they heard the news.

The immediate area surrounding the burnt remains of Snowflake's hut became the center of frantic searching. Villagers joined in, sensing the urgency that radiated from the adventurers and the dwarves. Though seemingly at peace, the enchanted forest held echoes of concern as the group scoured every nook and cranny for any sign of Swift.

Ben, leading the search party, called out, "Swift! Where are you?" His voice, echoing through the trees, carried a mix of command and concern. Memories of his upbringing in a village renowned for its strategic thinkers and scholars flashed through his mind. Ben's father, a revered leader, had instilled in him the importance of courage and wisdom. As a child, Ben had often explored the nearby forests, learning to read the land and understand its secrets. Now, those lessons guided his steps and decisions.

Snowflake, her eyes darting between the trees, spoke to the other dwarves in hushed tones. "He might be scared or confused. We need to find him before he gets too far."

The sun, descending in the sky, cast long shadows over the enchanted forest, intensifying the urgency of the search. The adventurers, the villagers, and the dwarves combed through the underbrush, their gazes flickering between the dense foliage and the charred remnants of Snowflake's hut.

As they ventured deeper into the forest, a subtle unease settled among the group. The absence of Swift became more ominous, and the realization that he might have taken something of significance with him heightened the stakes of the search.

Ava, her senses attuned to the magical currents in the air, paused. "I can feel a lingering trace of dark magic. It's faint, but it's there."

Holly, interpreting the gravity of Ava's words, urged the group to hasten their pace. "If Swift took a piece of the curse with him, we need to find him before the magic corrupts him or worse spreads to another town."

The enchanted forest, once a haven of mysteries and wonders, now echoed with the urgency of a quest. Shadows danced among the trees, and the air, tinged with the scent of magic, seemed to carry whispers of concern.

Snowflake, her eyes wide with fear, quickened her pace. "Swift! Please, we need to talk. Whatever you have, it's dangerous. We want to help."

Following Snowflake's lead, the adventurers pressed deeper into the enchanted realm. The surroundings became denser, the undergrowth more entwined, as if nature itself conspired to keep its secrets hidden. The lingering trace of dark magic guided them, a faint thread leading toward an uncertain destination.

As the group ventured further, the trees seemed to close around them, their branches intertwining like a cage. The village's sounds faded, replaced by the rustling of leaves and the occasional hoot of an unseen owl. The moonlight filtered through the canopy, casting shifting shadows that danced ominously on the forest floor. The atmosphere grew tense, the weight of their quest pressing upon them like a tangible force. Every step seemed to echo louder, and every whisper of the wind felt like the dark magic's breath on their necks.

Ava, her eyes fixed on the magical residue, spoke with a sense of urgency. "The trace is getting stronger. We're close."

The adventurers emerged into a small clearing, bathed in the moon's silvery glow filtering through the dense canopy. In the center stood Swift, his silhouette starkly contrasted against the ethereal light. He cradled a small, pulsating fragment in his hands – a captured piece of the dark magic.

Snowflake, her voice a plea, called out, "Swift, please! We don't know what that piece can do. Let us help you."

Swift, his eyes reflecting a mix of fear and insanity, hesitated. The magic within the fragment responded to the presence of the adventurers, flickering with an otherworldly glow.

Ben, stepping forward, spoke with a calming tone. "Swift, we're not here to harm you. We want to understand and help."

Tico, ever watchful, sensed the delicate balance of the situation. "If that piece is connected to the curse, we must handle it cautiously. It's not just Swift's well-being at stake; it's the safety of the entire village."

As the adventurers attempted to approach Swift, the fragment of dark magic reacted. The sky snapped with an ominous energy, and shadows danced with malevolent intent. Swift, his eyes wide with Panic, clutched the fragment tighter.

Ava, her senses alert, realized the peril. "This Magic is resisting us. We need to find a way to neutralize it without causing harm to Swift or the village."

Recalling the enchanted forest lore, Holly suggested, "There might be an ancient ritual, a way to sever the connection between Swift and the dark magic. We can't risk letting it spread."

Without hesitation, Swift turned on his heels and darted into the thicket of the forest once more. "Wait, Swift! We can't just let you face this alone," Snowflake called after him, her voice a blend of worry and resolve.

Tico, sensing Snowflake's internal struggle, offered a compassionate suggestion. "Snowflake, we'll catch up with Swift and bring him back safely. You don't have to bear this burden."

Snowflake hesitated, torn between the importance of the situation and her loyalty to Swift. "But I can't just stand by. He needs me," she insisted, a flicker of defiance in her eyes.

Ben, understanding her predicament, spoke with a deliberate tone. "Snowflake, we'll do everything we can to bring Swift back unharmed. Trust us to handle this. Your strength is needed back in the village, for now."

Reluctantly, Snowflake nodded, her internal struggle evident. "Just... bring him back, please," she implored, her voice soft yet filled with urgency.

With that, the adventurers set off into the thicket, determined to both rescue Swift and neutralize the dark magic's threat. Snowflake, torn between loyalty and the safety of the village, watched them disappear into the shadows, her heart heavy with worry.

As the party forged ahead to find Swift, Ben cast a lingering glance back at Snowflake, her expression etched with worry as she turned toward the village clearing. "We cannot allow Swift or that captured fragment to roam freely," he asserted, his gaze fixed on the vanishing figure of Snowflake behind the thicket. The weight of their mission bore heavily in his eyes. "We've witnessed the dire consequences of the curse. We cannot permit its further spread."

Tico voiced the tactical aspect of their mission. "Swift is familiar with the terrain. Tracking him won't be easy, but we have to move quickly. Every moment counts."

The trail left by Swift, and the captured fragment was faint, like whispers among the leaves. Still, the artifacts in their possession resonated with an otherworldly echo that guided their path.

As they ventured deeper into the enchanted woods, the atmosphere changed. The trees, their branches interwoven like a living tapestry, seemed to hold the echoes of untold tales. The air, tinged with the scent of ancient moss and the faint hum of mystical energies, whispered secrets only the oldest trees could comprehend.

Ava, her eyes glinting with magical insight, remarked, "The forest itself is guiding us. It recognizes the threat and yearns for balance."

Her fingers delicately traced over the leaves, as though engaged in a silent conversation with the towering ancients. Holly murmured, "The curse disrupted the natural order. We're here to restore it, to prevent further harm."

Their journey became a delicate dance between following the trail and deciphering the subtle cues the enchanted forest provided. The ancient trees, their gnarled roots weaving patterns on the forest floor, seemed to bend and sway in a rhythmic acknowledgment of the adventurers' quest.

After what felt like hours of traversing the ever-changing landscape, the trail led them to a clearing bathed in the soft glow of moonlight. In the center stood Swift again, his silhouette blending with the shadows of the surrounding trees—the captured fragment pulsed in his hands, its malevolent energy casting an eerie aura.

"Swift," Ben called out, his voice a gentle plea. "We're not here to fight. We want to help you and to understand. What drove you to take that fragment?"

Swift, his eyes wide with fear and confusion, hesitated. The magic within the fragment responded to the presence of the adventurers, flickering with an otherworldly glow. His mind was a battlefield, memories of camaraderie and laughter clashing with the dark whispers that now clouded his thoughts. "I just wanted to protect everyone," he muttered, his voice breaking. "But now... I don't know what's real anymore." The fragment pulsed, reflecting his inner turmoil, casting shadows across his face.

Tico, ever vigilant, spoke with a firm command. "We need to secure that fragment. It's a danger to you and everyone in the village. Let us help you break free from its influence."

As the adventurers approached, Swift took a step back, his gaze shifting between the captured fragment and the determined faces of his companions. The tension in the air became palpable, the moment hanging on the precipice of a decision that could shape the fate of the enchanted forest.

Ava, her magical senses attuned to the energy emanating from the fragment, noted, "The dark Magic is resisting. We need to act now, or it might unleash its power."

Swift, his eyes wide with the internal struggle between reason and the dark magic's seduction, took a step back. His hands trembled as the malevolent force tightened its grip on his mind. The adventurers, their senses attuned to the mystical undercurrents, witnessed Swift's futile attempts to resist.

"I... I can't," Swift muttered, his voice strained with the weight of the unseen battle within. "It's too strong. It's calling me."

Ava stepped forward, reflecting a mix of concern and dedication. "Resist it. We can help you."

Delving into the arcane intricacies of dark magic, Holly added, " The ritual must have been flawed. The forest didn't cleanse itself. The remnants of the dark magic are ever present, seeking fresh vessels."

Tico urged Swift, "Fight it, dwarf. Running won't solve anything. You're not alone in this."

Yet, the allure of the dark magic proved too potent for Swift to resist. In a moment of despair, Swift turned and fled into the depths of the enchanted forest, his silhouette disappearing among the shadows. The adventurers, their shared resolve solidifying, took off after him, their footsteps echoing through the silent woods. Before their pursuit, a disconcerting realization settled in—Swift exhibited unsettling signs of descending into insanity, a haunting reminder of the same madness that had afflicted the people of Perlitan.

The chase became a race between the adventurers and the elusive darkness that now possessed Swift. Once a sanctuary, the enchanted forest seemed to warp into an ever-shifting labyrinth, challenging the adventurers at every turn.

"Swift!" Ben called out, his voice echoing through the twisted branches. "We can help you break free. Don't succumb to the darkness!"

Ava's magical senses probed the environment. He added, "He's heading towards the heart of the forest. That's where the magic is strongest."

As they pursued Swift, the enchanted forest seemed to close around them, the trees growing denser and more oppressive. Shadows darted among the trunks, creating the illusion of figures moving just out of sight. The echoes of their footsteps merged with the whispering of leaves, producing an eerie, almost musical resonance that heightened their sense of urgency. Every rustle and crack seemed amplified, each one a reminder of the malevolent force they were up against.

That same force clung to Swift's mind pulsing with an unsettling rhythm, leading them deeper into the unknown in a cunning cat-and-mouse game.

The adventurers, at last, arrived at a clearing in the heart of the forest. Swift stood at its center, his silhouette bathed in an eerie glow, a manifestation of the dark magic enveloping him like a sinister cloak that seemed to be expanding and intensifying with every passing moment.

"Swift, we've come to help," Holly implored, her eyes scanning the magical currents. "Let us break the chains that bind you."

But Swift, his eyes vacant, spoke with an otherworldly voice that resonated with the dark magic's influence. "You cannot stop what has begun. The forest yearns for its true power to be unleashed."

A surge of dark energy emanated from Swift, forming into tendrils that lashed out at the adventurers. Tico, his reflexes honed by years of combat training in the harsh landscapes of his homeland, pushed his companions aside, taking the brunt of the magical assault. Memories of training under his stern mentor, learning the art of agility and resilience, flashed through his mind. Wincing in pain, he staggered back, his thoughts momentarily drifting to the family he had vowed to protect, physically battered but resolute.

The adventurers, fueled by a sense of urgency, wasted no time. Ben, Ava, and Holly rushed to Tico's aid, checking on his condition. Tico, though visibly battered, assured them he could press on.

Their momentary diversion allowed Swift to slip further away, his silhouette flickering like a ghost ahead. With Tico stabilized, the group resumed their pursuit, but each attempt to catch up felt like grasping at elusive shadows in the ever-darkening forest.

Her breath forming mist in the chill, Holly shouted, "Swift! Please, wait!"

But Swift, driven by an unseen force, pressed on, his figure melding with the shifting darkness. Ben, a mix of worry and persistence etched on his face, led the pursuit, his instincts guiding him through the labyrinth of trees.

As they approached the outskirts of the enchanted forest, the terrain transformed. The towering trees gave way to a clearing, and in the distance rose a mysterious tower, its spires reaching toward the sky like ancient watchmen.

In the distance, they could make out the silhouette of Swift, looking up at a towering structure. "Let down your hair!" the adventurers heard Swift shout.

Within seconds, a rope-like ladder emerged from the top of the tower while slowly descending toward Swift. The adventurers watched in confusion and disbelief as Swift climbed up the ladder toward an open window at the top of the tower…

Epilogue

In a moment of revelation, Swift's voice pierced the stillness of the forest, a desperate plea reverberating through the clearing. "Let down your hair!" His cry hung in the air, a poignant invocation that seemed to stir the very essence of the ancient tower.

For a breathless pause, silence enveloped the scene, broken only by the whispering of leaves and the distant nocturnal symphony of the forest. Then, as if compelled by Swift's petition, a figure materialized at a high window, bathed in the ethereal glow of moonlight.

Swift's breath caught in his throat as he beheld the spectral vision above. The girl, with her flowing mane of luminescent hair, appeared almost ethereal against the backdrop of the night. Each strand shimmered like spun silver, catching the moon's radiance in a mesmerizing dance that held the onlookers spellbound.

With a graceful motion, the girl fashioned her radiant locks into a makeshift rope, offering it as a lifeline to Swift below.

Seizing the opportunity with unwavering resolve, Swift embarked on his ascent, his movements fluid and deliberate despite the perilous climb. With each foothold gained, he drew closer to the mysterious girl above, driven by an unyielding determination to uncover the secrets concealed within the tower's ancient confines.

As Swift approached the window, an unspoken connection flickered between him and the girl. Their eyes wove a tale of complex emotions, bridging shared fears and unexpressed desires. A fragile bond tightened, saturating the atmosphere with a palpable sense of mystery and anticipation.

With one last burst of resolve, Swift breached the window, vanishing into the shadows that embraced the tower's interior. The girl, her eyes fixed on the now empty opening, exhaled a breath she hadn't been aware of holding. Her face, a blend of apprehension and subtle relief, mirrored the enigma left in Swift's wake.

As the girl withdrew into the sanctuary of the tower, drawing her radiant hair back into its ethereal embrace, a sense of foreboding settled over the clearing. In the heart of the forest, the dark magic captured in the bottle yearned to be reunited with its remnants that now made a home for itself in a tower where a girl with long hair lived...

About the Author

N. Alessandro Penington is an award-winning American author who grew up in Detroit, MI. He has served in the military for over 16 years and has been on multiple deployments. He holds a DBA in Business, and He loves to use his experiences to guide him while he writes and brings fun, family, and riveting fantasy stories to life.

In his spare time, N. Alessandro loves to cook, write, work on cars and hang out with his family, his amazing veteran girlfriend and their 2 boys. While working in the entertainment industry for over eight years and being heavily involved and acting in live theater has expanded his imagination. He uses parts of everything that he has lived to build the world he creates.

"Words are the foundation of everything; the stories we make with them are the building blocks that allow people to dream" - N. Alessandro Penington.

Connect with N. Alessandro Penington:

Website: SeerendipPublishing.com
Facebook: N. Alessandro Penington
Instagram: @NAlessandroPenington

Don't Miss The Other Books in This Series

Book 1: The Rose in the Glass Dome

Prepare for an exhilarating plunge into a realm of magic and menace with "The Rose in the Glass Dome." Join four fearless adventurers on a mission to rescue Rose from the clutches of darkness, only to find themselves ensnared in a web of intrigue that threatens to unleash chaos upon the kingdom. This heart-pounding saga weaves a spellbinding tapestry of danger and daring, promising an electrifying journey where the stakes are high, and every twist ignites the imagination. Brace yourself for an epic adventure that will leave you breathless and yearning for more.

www.ingramcontent.com/pod-product-compliance
Lightning Source LLC
Chambersburg PA
CBHW041053310726
48978CB00011BA/533